Olivia's Journey

Latrina R. Graves McCarty

WestBow
PRESS®
A DIVISION OF THOMAS NELSON
& ZONDERVAN

This is a work of fiction. All of the characters, names, incidents,
organizations, and dialogue in this novel are either the products
of the author's imagination or are used fictitiously.

WestBow Press books may be ordered through booksellers or by contacting:

WestBow Press
A Division of Thomas Nelson & Zondervan
1663 Liberty Drive
Bloomington, IN 47403
www.westbowpress.com
1 (866) 928-1240

ISBN: 978-1-9736-4090-5 (sc)
ISBN: 978-1-9736-4091-2 (hc)
ISBN: 978-1-9736-4089-9 (e)

Library of Congress Control Number: 2018911495

Print information available on the last page.

WestBow Press rev. date: 10/8/2018

Contents

Dedication

This book is dedicated to my late husband,
LaRue F. McCarty (1970–2010).

I know you are so proud of me. I know you are watching me every day. I want to thank you for teaching me right from wrong. And you know what? I love you so, so, so much. I know you know it. People will miss you so much, but I would rather have you not suffering so you can be in heaven with God. I am not jealous because I want to remind people of you. You did a lot of things for people. And I remember you telling me all the time, "You can tell your daddy anything" And that is what I am doing now.

So, to shorten time, I would like to say,
"Thank you for everything! And see you in heaven!"

Love, your daughter,
Ana (age seven)

Take it all one day at a time and enjoy the journey.

—Kristi Bartlett

Chapter 1

Starting Line

Hope is not a resting place but a starting point—a cactus, not a cushion.

—H. Jackson Brown Jr.

Dr. Olivia Journey Douglas Bentley could not exactly remember when she finally let go and completely let God be God of every area of her life. She had grown weary of trying to change people or make them into the image she wanted them to be or thought they should be. Olivia remembered the day so vividly when she received an awful message from a guy calling her the B word. His life was no means ideal, but he was someone she could settle with. He basically told her to lose his contact by texting, "Don't ever beg for a friendship or relationship with anyone. If you don't receive the same effort you give out, then let them go."

She thought she had a chance because for a year he was reading her heartfelt messages and responding occasionally. She was so happy before that message. She was even more devastated because his birthday was coming up in a week. She was plotting to send him the perfect gift. She had sent him something a few months before.

It was a nice gift basket. She was so excited, but he never responded with a "Thank you" or "I got it." Olivia still pursued him, for she felt a tug in her heart that she had never experienced before, even at the age of forty-five. She did, in fact, have her reservations, and she did message him, "Goodbye" on several occasions. Now she thought she might have done more to try to get a reaction from him. When he responded with "Okay, and it is for the best," a few minutes later, she would change her mind. It was not as if he did not tell her directly that he did not want a relationship, but she felt as if they could at least be friends. She thought a friendship would lead to more one day.

Olivia was an independent woman who was able to spoil herself. There were times when she thought she wanted a companion, but those feelings would pass just as quickly as they would surface. Why was she going to settle for him? Her life was not over. She was smart and beautiful and grossed about $500,000 annually as an adjunct, seasonal college professor, a director of her own nonprofit agency, and an author of screenplays and novels, as well as occasional speaking engagements. She was not rich, but she did not want for anything that she could not provide for herself. Her children were independent as well; she had just moved her youngest into her dormitory a few weeks earlier.

It was not time for Olivia to get a roommate. It was time for her to get to know Olivia Journey Douglas Bentley, doctor of philosophy, with limited responsibilities. Yes, she missed all the perks of a relationship. But why was she willing to settle for mediocre?

Sitting on her lanai, she was reminiscing and thinking how grateful she was. She decided to sell her home a few months after her daughter finally chose an Ivy League school in another state. Isabella had been telling her since she was old enough to know anything about everything she wanted her mom to go with her even if she decided to attend a school miles away. Isabella's mind changed when she started visiting college campuses during her junior year of high school. Isabella was so convincing that Olivia allowed her to go on an overnight visit with another parent as a chaperon. Olivia knew Isabella was more mature than anyone her age, but as a mom, she was still concerned. Olivia knew then that her baby girl would eventually develop her own wings and soar like Dr. Olivia Journey Douglas Bentley had taught both of her children to do. She did miss her children but knew they both would do exceptionally well at whatever they put their hands to do.

Olivia put her feet up on her patio ottoman to extend her five-foot, eight-inch frame. She was quite pleased with her patio sectional; she knew exactly what she wanted. She knew how she wanted to relax after a long day at work or a tough workout with her personal trainer or if she wanted to simply enjoy the scenery. This was why she fell in love at first sight with her new home. Her Realtor and best friend, Ava, suggested similar condos because she felt Olivia would be tempted to get lonely in trying to occupy three thousand square feet. Olivia did consider that idea but then ignored it. She smiled to herself.

Thinking back to his message... It was not easy being told that she was not wanted, but she knew she was a catch for the right one. Even if she was destined to be single for the rest of her life, she would be happy. Besides, she definitely knew how to spoil herself. She closed her eyes, lost in her own thoughts.

Olivia heard a knock at the door and woke up. It had to be the delivery person for her dinner that she had ordered earlier.

The sun was setting. On days like this, she was grateful for her home choice. This building was the only one with more than one restaurant. She got up and went to find her purse in the bedroom so she could give a tip, but then realized she was only wearing her bathrobe. She had taken a late shower after her trainer, Antonio, felt the need to torture her for two and a half hours. She had not worked out with him in seven days. She thought about firing him because he was straight crazy, but then she realized that she needed *crazy* to keep her focused. She had gained twenty unexplained pounds of emotional stress.

The doorbell rang again. Olivia slipped into her favorite yoga pants and T-shirt. Her shirt was heather gray with a silver Nike swoosh and the words "Shut Up and Run." The pants were black with the matching symbol. She thought it minimized her full, size 14 hips. She noticed that the pants were a little loose. She smiled to herself.

Olivia rushed to the door with money in hand. After she opened it, she saw her favorite delivery guy, Miguel. Miguel was from Nigeria and a graduate student in internal medicine. He was hoping to apply to the top medical school in the country in a few months. They normally caught up on the latest news in his home country every time he delivered her food, but today, she was famished. She had not eaten since her lean smoothie this morning.

"Hi, Miguel. How is it going?"

"Good evening, Dr. Journey," he said in his thick Nigerian accent. Miguel had been in the United States for three years, but anyone would think that he'd just moved to the US yesterday. "And how have you been?" he added.

"I am so hungry. I forgot I was on a diet until you got here," Olivia said.

They both laughed. Olivia invited him in for a coffee smoothie, which was his usual when he came, but he declined.

"I have got to get these deliveries out; I have a study group later this evening," he said. "And I know you are hungry."

"That I am!" Olivia said, laughing. "Before you leave tell me: how is your family?"

"They are well; however, they say they miss me." He smiled. "They are anxious for me to return. It is my hope to return permanently in three years, for I plan to do my residency in Nigeria. I cannot wait to see them when I visit in two weeks. I miss my mom's cooking."

They laughed again. Olivia knew how he felt about American foods. He reminded her constantly how she should hire a chef because all foods were better prepared by your own hands and for the simple fact that you knew exactly what you were consuming. She was seriously taking it into consideration. Since she had started her adjunct position for the summer term, her time had been quite limited. She was seriously considering giving up the teaching position altogether. It was worse than being a middle school teacher. She taught secondary education for years before she was able to establish her nonprofit agency.

"Okay," Olivia said. "But wait. I have something for you." Olivia knew how tight funds were for Miguel, even though he had a full academic scholarship to graduate school. She knew that everything he received went to his parents and siblings. So basic needs for him were luxuries.

"Dr. J., you did not have to," he said.

"I know, but just allow me to do this for you." Olivia went into her study and pulled out of her top draw a $250 gift card to Walmart. She reentered the room and gave Miguel the card.

"Thank you, Dr. J.," he said sheepishly. "May your God continue to bless you even more than He already has."

"I receive that, Miguel, and thank you," Olivia added.

They moved to the door together.

"Thank you, again, Dr. J.," Miguel said. "And please consider hiring a chef."

"I will, and have a good study session and home visit if I do not see you before then."

"Thank you, and I will."

Oliva closed the door behind him and locked it. Even though the building had a concierge service as well as an awesome security team, she still found herself cautious. Maybe it was because she had decided to try her hand at writing mysteries. She smiled. Who would have thought she would be an author of anything?

The sounds of hunger and the smell distracted her thoughts. Olivia had thought about hiring a chef, but now, her thoughts were on devouring her favorite meal from her favorite eatery, The

Cheesecake Factory. Even though she had temporarily given up cheesecake, she could not get enough of their freshly grilled salmon with asparagus and mashed potatoes. Olivia also ordered their specialty wheat bread with butter even though she knew she should not have. She thought, *At least I did not order my favorite, a slice of lemon meringue cheesecake.*

She prepared her plate and decided on a glass of sparkling water with lemon instead of what she really wanted, a Coke Zero. Olivia also grabbed silverware and a napkin and went back to enjoy the view from her lanai. The wind had picked up, so the waves were a sight to behold. Sometimes she would find herself in a trance, for the waves were hypnotizing.

She thought of him as she sat. She wondered what he was doing at this very moment. She was tempted to message him. She was still excited when he read her messages, but she knew that, at this point, it did not really matter. He had never even paid her a visit, nor did he ever invite her anywhere. She remembered some of their chance visits. With everything she had to offer, she still was baffled by his reluctance and his message. Why did he send such an awful message? Even though he tried to explain it to her, she chose not to read his lengthy explanation. One of her girlfriends told her early on that he just did not like her. With that, she dismissed her imposing thoughts, prayed over her food, and enjoyed her meal as she listened to the sounds of the waves. It would be dark soon, but she was determined to go on her evening walk. Besides, she was not as exhausted as she normally was after a long week, but she knew that she needed to get going if she wanted to beat nightfall. She had visited the gym earlier; she was simply enjoying all of the amities her building offered, but now, she simply wanted to get out and walk the shoreline.

Again she thought of him, but she was determined to move beyond what she did not understand because it was a waste of time. She quickly tidied up her kitchen, changed into some workout clothing with socks and shoes, and grabbed her phone, earbuds, and keys with change wallet attached. She stopped right before leaving because she felt like she was forgetting something. She considered it and but then left. She was determined to walk for at least thirty minutes, because she knew that her night was not over. She had to deal with the care of her natural hair. She sighed and smiled simultaneously as she made her way to the elevator. She disliked elevators; however, she was in a hurry and had no time to use the stairs. She pressed the down button and waited. When the elevator opened, she froze. It was *him* with a *her.* Olivia's mind traveled back twenty-four and a half years.

"I have met the man!" Olivia said with a giggle to her suite mates.

She had never in her life said that about anyone she had ever admired. Olivia was a twenty-two-year-old senior in college. She was expected to graduate in two months. The majority of her friends were seriously dating, and some were even engaged, but Olivia always seemed to attach herself to the wrong men. Once she actually discovered who they were, she still seemed to manage to linger a little longer even after the "relationship" had run its course. Her biggest issue was trying to change the individual, although she did not want to admit it.

Olivia's parents divorced when she was in her preteens. She had a natural father and a stepfather. However, neither one of them, she thought, measured up to her definition of a dad. She liked boys, but she was always afraid of them not liking her back. She would allow the males in her life to define her by adjusting to what she thought they wanted.

Olivia was devastated when he did not call her for three days after he asked for her phone number. When he finally called, they talked for hours and made plans to meet the next day. He had invited her over to his parents' home. Later Olivia discovered that he was only visiting his parents for a few weeks and was scheduled to go back to California to establish his residence. He had just been honorably discharged from the United States Air Force. Olivia was always fascinated by a man in uniform.

Now, standing here looking at the man who called her the B word getting off the elevator with a her, Olivia knew then that *this* guy had to be added to the category of the wrongs in her life. He spoke first.

"Hi, Olivia, how are you?" he asked. "Do you live in this building?"

"Yes, I am doing well," she replied. Olivia started to feel her pulse race, and she was not anywhere near a finish line.

"Oh, this is my cousin, Angel. Her twin brother, Aaron, just moved into this building and invited us to see his new place," he said.

Even though she felt relieved to hear that it was only his cousin, she still felt distant. It was a familiar feeling. She knew then that she was over him. It felt good. She finally felt free of him.

Looking at Angel, she said, "Well, I know your brother is loving his new place, because I definitely am."

"That is all he has been talking about," she said. "We are here because I want to see it for myself."

"Well, he is definitely not exaggerating." Olivia said with a smile.

Olivia began to walk into the elevator, and Angel walked into the hall. He was not moving. He stared a little longer.

"Angel, I will catch up with you," he said.

"Okay, cuz. You have the address, right?" she added.

"Yes," he replied.

Angel proceeded down the hallway.

"What's up?" Olivia asked.

"I just wanted to make sure that you were okay. I know how it feels to love someone, and they do not love you back in the same way," he said.

"Are you serious?" Olivia asked. "I am fine; in fact, I am doing great."

"You honestly look great," he said. He looked at her admiringly.

He was holding the elevator's hold button. It signaled. "Why don't I ride down with you, so we can talk?" he asked.

"Why?" Olivia said.

She was beginning to become annoyed. Why would she want to continue this conversation with him? He was beginning to look very unattractive the more he spoke. At this point, she did not even know why she even liked him to begin with. She admitted that she did have a problem lusting after men who were over six-foot-three.

"I just want to make sure that you are okay with me choosing not to talk to you," he said.

"You already told me several times to get lost," Olivia said. She was getting angry. Who in the world did he think he was? "I really am doing great, and I am trying to catch an evening walk before the night falls."

"Maybe we can walk together," he said.

"Again, why?" Olivia said in a more elevated tone of voice.

"I want to tell you why …"

Olivia interrupted him. "Please get off the elevator. Just like there are other people who need this elevator, there are other people out there for both of us. You are not all that! Please, get off this elevator."

He got off, and Olivia hurriedly pressed the button for the lobby on the key panel. She was trying to compose her anger before the doors closed, but she made certain that he heard her say, "How stuck-on-stupid can you be?"

She felt her face growing warm. Then she thought about how much an idiot she must have been to even like him. What nerve! How was he even going to fix his mouth to say anything to her? He could not have cared less how she felt a month ago. She knew then and there that she wanted to be alone. She needed to be alone. She wanted to feel comfortable in her singleness. She had thought about contacting the previous guy she had actually fallen in love with about two years into her singleness, but this evening, she knew that she was done with all of them. Dumb! It was dumb to think that she could control or change anyone. Why was she constantly choosing to stay on this circular ride? She had graduated from the carousel to the roller coaster, but it was still the same. She always ended up right where she began.

Olivia made her way to the lobby and out of the back entry, which led to the beach. From the looks of the sun, she was grateful that she still had at least about one full hour of sunlight left to walk. She thought about her encounter with him. Olivia admitted that she was an emotional binge eater, for she even thought about going to the newly opened frozen custard shop that many have been raving about. She smiled because sometimes she could even convince herself that it was okay to eat wrong. However, she had a renewed strength, and she refused to allow anything or anyone to distract her. She knew then that Floyd Alexander Ferguson V was not going to ever again waste any more of her time in her thoughts.

She paused to practice a few stretches that her trainer had shown her earlier and began to walk along the beach. She adjusted her playlist to her favorite Christian rapper and smelled the air which was consumed with a combination of fried seafood and all types of grilled red meats. She was excited because she was not tempted to even stop at her favorite coffee shop. She was a woman who was determined to simply walk with a clear mind; she craved peace and some sanity.

About fifteen minutes in the walk, she tried to adjust her playlist. She saw a message from Floyd: "I just want to make sure you are okay."

She felt herself warm again. She thought, *What is his problem? He is not saying anything about getting to know each other on a deeper level or even apologizing, but he is wondering if I am okay. Why? It has been one month!*

Olivia deleted the message and continued to walk. Again, she refused to allow anything to stop her momentum! She turned off her phone and walked in peace. It was a Saturday night. She had not been on a date in about three years. She and Floyd had never gotten to that point. She still was uncertain as to how she had become so attached to him when she rarely saw him. Maybe she was so convinced that he was the one that she refused to stop and think how ridiculous it was. Olivia prided herself on logical thinking, but this was pure insanity.

She looked down at her watch and realized that she had to turn around if she had any chance of getting home before night finally fell. It had been a long day, and she was looking forward to soaking in her oversized, jetted tub and reading a novel she had started last night. She was also excited about attending her sister's church the next day. Her sister's dance team was ministering, and they ushered in the spirit so boldly. Olivia needed a reprieve right now.

The sun was almost gone when she got home. She saw Floyd and his cousins, but they did not see her. She quickly walked into the entrance and was about to open the door to the staircase when she heard her name. She was not sure who was calling her, if they were calling her, but she opened the door and sprinted all the way to her eighth-floor condo. She was panting. Just as she was closing the door to her home, there was a knock. She opened the door and was prepared to cuss Floyd out. She never used profanity, but she was going to use it this day. Olivia stopped and was surprised. It was Jacque, the bellhop.

"I am sorry, Jacque. I thought you were someone else," Olivia said.

"I would hate to be that person," Jacque said sheepishly. "These came for you earlier today. Apparently, they forgot to deliver them."

He was holding a large crimson box wrapped in the prettiest ivory ribbon she had ever seen in one hand. At first it seemed as if it were a wrapped garment. In the other hand, he was holding a single rose in what appeared to be a pure crystal vase. Olivia was shocked, for she had not received roses since her twelfth wedding anniversary. She remembered that day so vividly. She received thirteen red roses. Her husband had sent an extra one to symbolize the expectation of another year. They were delivered to her on her job. Suddenly, she felt a pang of guilt because she remembered how she took her marriage for granted. She was lost in her thoughts until she heard Jacque ask, "Where should I place these items, Dr. Bentley?"

"Yes, thanks, on the kitchen counter, please," Olivia said.

She was able to read the card from the box before Jacques placed the items on the counter: "You are who God created you to be. Do not allow anything or anyone to distract you. God made no mistake when He created you, for He created you in His image."

She was puzzled. She had no clue who could be sending her anything. Who would take out the time to do this for her? Yes, she was a great catch to someone in her own eyes, but through the eyes of many men she had admired over the years, not so much. Jacque was waiting. She went to her room to get his gratuity. She thanked him, and he left.

She opened the box and saw seven roses. She was lost in her thoughts until she noticed another card attached to the single rose in the crystal vase. She took note of the red ribbon as it intertwined with the same ivory ribbon color pattern from the packaged roses.

The second card read, "Be still, for in time, you will know."

Olivia was surprised because she was still wanted to be a part of her life, but she had no clue who would send such an elaborate gift. They were nice, so she placed all of the roses in the single vase. She wondered at the symbolism, but then remembered she had so much to do; it was nearly 8:00 p.m. She prepared her oversized jetted tub. Her body ached; she honestly could not figure out why she decided to run this evening. Then she realized that she was trying to run away from total embarrassment of liking someone more than she liked herself. Lesson learned.

Around 11:00 p.m., Olivia was scanning some files that she had been avoiding all weekend. She noticed that her phone was off from her run. She read text messages from both of her children and her grandma, mom, and twin sister and responded to each. Then she noticed a message from Floyd, again. She decided not to even read the message, for she had had enough. She blocked his social media page. She had to do it for herself. She needed time to digest him out of her system. It was time for her to begin her journey of restoring what she had so easily given up—her self-worth.

Olivia knew in her heart then that she really did not care who her admirer was, for she was discovering that she was falling in love with herself all over again.

Chapter 2

————————— ❦ —————————

Ready

The soul should always stand ajar ready to welcome
the ecstatic experience.

—Emily Dickinson

Normally Olivia ran late to church but not today. She even was
able to visit the gym that morning. She felt refreshed and quite
revived. She was glad she decided to close the agency for an entire
week before the summer program was scheduled to begin; she also
gave her college students an online assignment. She really needed an
opportunity to regroup, and her children would be visiting midweek
for a few days. She really missed her son.

As she was looking in her closet to make her final wardrobe
selection, she remembered the day her son, Isaiah, told her that he
no longer enjoyed the game of baseball. He had been playing his
beloved sport since before he could even walk.

"Mom, I just do not love it," Isaiah said.

"Why not?" she protested.

"Mom, you are trying to live my life for me?" he added.

Olivia was shocked because she prided herself on never trying to live vicariously through her children. She knew many moms who pushed their children, especially in sports, so that they would be taken care of by the same children they gave birth to. It was sad. She reminded her children that she was educated, had a job, and could take care of herself and them too. Olivia knew her purpose was to leave her children an inheritance.

Olivia's thoughts were interrupted by the sound of an incoming text message. She knew it was her sister, Octavia. She looked at the time first and saw that she even had time to have coffee or try to blend a fruit smoothie. She read the message, and of course, it was from her sister. Octavia was asking if she was coming to church and also if she wanted to have dinner with her and William after the service.

Olivia thought about it. Octavia and William resembled newlyweds. They were a sight to behold. Olivia was so happy for her sister. She had been waiting for her Boaz for quite some time. Ironically, William had been waiting for just as long. Even though Octavia was inviting her to dinner, she knew how it would end up. Seeing them together would remind Olivia of thoughts she had been avoiding, especially during the holidays. Yes, Olivia loved interacting with family during the holidays, but on this Memorial Day weekend, she wanted nothing more to do than to enjoy the solace of her new surroundings. She wanted to walk the beach a little farther than yesterday. This time she actually wanted to stop at one of the creameries and enjoy a low-fat treat.

Olivia responded to her sister's message with a "maybe" and continued to get dressed. Maybe she would go to Octavia's for dinner. Olivia was just hoping that William and Octavia had given up the notion of trying to make a love connection for her. She honestly had enough from her grandmother, Olga, trying to hook her up with someone. Olivia's mom did ask her only once if she was ever planning on remarrying. Olivia smiled. She could honestly say that she was happy. She admitted that she did have her moments, but they were getting better. Today was a good day. Olivia paused. She remembered …

"Why don't we just take it one day at a time?" her boyfriend said, as they traveled down highway 49 south. It was their first rode trip together.

Olivia's nerves eased. "Okay," she said. He had this calming effect about him. Olivia honestly had never met anyone so patient, kind, and selfless …

Olivia's thoughts were interrupted by her alarm. Now she had no time to spare if she wanted to make herself a smoothie. Olivia showered, dressed, and prepared the ingredients for her smoothie. She knew she was pushing the time, but she knew that traffic was slow on any given Sunday morning. The recipe called for fresh coffee grains. Olivia decided then that she would begin her caffeine detox tomorrow! She already felt a headache trying to surface. She devoured the smoothie and finished dressing. She glanced at the time, gathered her things, and left. She was ready for whatever the day might hold!

Olivia was always fascinated by her sister's church. She had never seen so many superficial people in one setting. Yes, Olivia knew that she had no room to judge anyone, but she honestly did not get it. Yes, at times the word was "right on time," but not always.

Olivia looked around and saw William; he was all smiles as he watched his wife dance before the Lord during praise and worship. He looked so goofy, especially when it came to her sister. They both were obviously delirious about each other. Olivia was so happy for them. William spotted her and waved her over. Olivia took a seat beside him. William was about six-foot-three, but in her heels, Olivia was about as tall as he was. They embraced and smiled at Octavia as the dancers and the praise team ushered in God's presence. It was powerful. Olivia was touched and tried to hold back the tears, but they came. She surrendered.

The service was powerful. Olivia had agreed to have dinner with them. Olivia was on the most intense high until she saw Floyd headed their way. Before she had an opportunity to process the situation, he and William were shaking hands. She had not told anyone of her temporary infatuation with Floyd. It was too embarrassing to tell anyone, and she had forgotten he was a member of New Christian Faith Center.

"Olivia, this is my friend Floyd, and Floyd, this is my sister-in-law, Olivia." William said. William and Octavia were grinning from ear to ear. What was going on? Did Floyd have anything to do with this?

"We invited Floyd over for dinner too, if you do not mind," Octavia said casually.

Olivia prided herself for not using profanity, but she wanted to cuss right there in church. What in the world was going on? Through her frustration, she glanced at Floyd, who seemed just as confused and embarrassed as she was. Olivia also saw that William and Octavia had no idea what was going on because they were looking starry-eyed at each other.

Floyd spoke first. "I thought we were simply going over the plans for the new sports complex to present to the board."

"We are, but we have to eat," William said as he was coming out of his trance with his wife.

"Yes, and I invited Olivia, who is familiar with these deals because she runs a successful nonprofit agency, which has a smaller-scale sports program," Octavia said proudly.

Octavia and William had no clue. Olivia could not break their hearts.

She looked at Floyd and said, "I would be more than happy to assist, but I only have a few hours to spare."

William and Octavia looked a little guilty, but they acted like they did not even care about getting caught for trying to make a match—a match that would not be. Olivia vowed then that she would never try to match souls.

Dinner was great. Her sister had always been an excellent cook and had gotten better since she married William a little over two years ago. Her sister was great being single, but she was the greatest married. She had become comfortable in her single life, so when William came along, he had a tough time wooing her into his arms. When they were dating, it was something out of a comic book. She played so hard to get, and it almost drove him away. Olivia still could not understand to this day why she did not want to admit that she fell in love with William at first sight. They both did.

"Olivia?" Octavia was trying to grab her attention.

"Olivia, what do you think about the plans?" Floyd asked.

Olivia was quite impressed with the plans. She admitted that she and Floyd did not get the opportunity to know each other before he pushed her away. He seemed incredibly smart.

"I am actually quite impressed, and I think your board would love it." Olivia said.

"See, I told you, man, that it was good," William said.

"You did," Floyd said. "Thank you, Olivia."

"No problem," Olivia said.

"Anyone for dessert?" Octavia asked.

Before anyone could respond, William and Octavia hurried into the kitchen. It was obvious what their intentions were.

Floyd spoke first. "I did not know they were trying to make a match," Floyd said.

"Me either, but too bad they do not know that you dislike me, and after last night, the feelings are mutual," Olivia said.

"Olivia …"

"Stop, let us just play along. They will never know," Olivia said and looked at her watch. The sun would be setting soon, and she wanted to walk as far up the shoreline as possible before the night fell.

Floyd sensed her urgency. "Do you have plans?"

"As a matter of fact, I do," Olivia confirmed.

"Why don't we act like we hit it off and leave together?" Floyd suggested.

Olivia thought that was the best thing that had come out of his month since last night.

"Yes, great idea," Olivia said with a smile. She knew then that Floyd was not going to be anywhere in her life. She was sad that she had ever thought that he could be the one.

Octavia and William reentered the dining room. William was carrying vanilla ice cream while Octavia was carrying Patty LaBelle's peach cobbler. Olivia smiled. Even though Octavia could throw down main courses, she was not a baker.

Floyd stood up first, and Olivia followed him.

"Octavia and William, thank you for inviting me. The food was to die for, Octavia, but you know I am watching my figure," Floyd said as he placed his hands on his imaginary pot belly. Floyd was super fine, standing about six-foot-six tall. He was a giant in the gym. That Olivia knew. Floyd glanced at Olivia, who was a little starry-eyed herself.

Regaining her composure, Olivia said, "Yes, as always, sis, you are a great cook, but I am trying to beat the sun setting."

Floyd interrupted and said, "Yes, Olivia has promised to take me on her shoreline adventure."

Olivia was becoming quite irritated with Floyd. Why was he lying? There was no way she was going to allow this to happen. Was he serious? This lie was extreme.

Octavia and William looked overjoyed, and this time, they were not hiding their approval. "Yes, Olivia, that would be an awesome idea," Octavia exclaimed. "Why don't you and Floyd leave now, so you can see the sun set, for it is a beautiful view from Olivia's lanai?"

Olivia thought that Octavia had lost her mind. Floyd saw Olivia's expression and quickly intervened.

"Yes, my cousin lives in that same building and simply raves about his view of the ocean," Floyd said. "Olivia, thank you for inviting me."

Olivia thought that she was about to lose her mind up in here.

Again, Floyd tried to intervene, but Olivia cut him off this time. She had enough of the lies that were coming out of his mouth. What were his motives? Regardless, she'd had enough and was ready to leave his presence. She knew he did not expect her to invite him along for a walk and definitely not into her home.

Olivia got up from the dining room table, and Floyd followed her lead. Olivia noticed Octavia giving William a high five, and as always, the goofy smiles were never ending with these two.

Olivia hugged them both, and Floyd hugged Octavia and gave William a high five. Olivia did not understand any of this. Was this all a set-up? Was Floyd also involved? This was too much for her. She wanted to question Floyd, but she did not even want to be around him at this point. He was quite smart and handsome, but his apparent stupidity was way too much for her to handle.

Floyd opened the door for Olivia as he walked out onto the front porch of Octavia and William's five thousand–square-foot colonial-style home. Their porch was always warm and welcoming on any given day, even during the worst winter storm. The porch reminded Olivia of summer days with Grandma Olga. Grandma Olga always loved shelling and snapping any types of vegetables. Olivia and Octavia enjoyed all of the stories she would tell. Octavia always wanted a porch like Grandma Olga's to remind her of the importance of family.

Yes, Olivia had a family once. She was able to enjoy her husband and her then-young children. Now the only thing she wanted to do was to enjoy her singlehood without some guy playing around like he was still in high school. Olivia could take care of herself and was ready to be alone for the rest of her life to avoid her attention being divided with any type of distraction.

Olivia and Floyd made their way to their cars in silence. Olivia refused to even look his way until Octavia and William closed the door.

Once the door was closed and Olivia knew they were safe to

speak without anyone listening, she spoke sternly through clenched teeth. Floyd stepped back and froze as Olivia spoke. Olivia even surprised herself.

"I do not know what you told them or why you even hinted to them that we were going to take this any further than my sister's driveway. You have made it perfectly clear that you wanted nothing to do with me, and I *be dog* if I want anything to do with you now," Olivia said, glaring.

While Floyd was yet frozen, Olivia got into her Range Rover and tried her best to not yield to temptation and run over him.

Olivia did not want this to completely cast a shadow on her day, but she could not stop replaying the entire day. Why would he do this? Olivia adjusted her playlist to her favorite Christian artists. She needed Jesus right now.

Olivia was trapped in her thoughts and could not even remember how she got to her parking garage.

"What a day!" she said to herself.

When she finally reached the lobby, she spotted both of her children, Isabella and Isaiah. Isabella ran ahead of her brother, and they all embraced. All of this confirmed to Olivia that life was worth it because of these two. When she looked at her children, she saw the only man who was able to capture her heart. Even though Olivia missed her life with her family, she knew now that she was ready for her next chapter. She was grateful for her children, who kept her focused. Isaiah struggled with all of Isabella's bags as they chatted all the way to her penthouse.

Olivia smiled. Her children were not scheduled to arrive until Wednesday, but she knew that she needed this reprieve. Her phone vibrated as she was unlocking her front door, and she knew it was Floyd. He wanted to talk again. Once inside, Olivia made her way to her bedroom as she heard Isabella and Isaiah arguing over the TV's remote control. She smiled again, took her shoes off, and walked out onto her lanai. She sat in her favorite recliner and texted him back. She contemplated copying and sending him the exact message he had sent her a month ago, but she knew that it was not in her character to do.

She wrote, "At this point, I wish that I had never sent you that first message. I am sorry for pursuing you. Please do not try to contact me, for I am fine; I am great actually. Goodbye."

Olivia did not care if she laid eyes on him again; she was ready with a renewed strength of boldness.

Chapter 3

.... * * * * * * * * * * * * * * * * ✦ ✤ ✦ * * * * * * * * * * * * * * * * ....

Attention Divided

When someone shows you who they are, believe them the first time.

—Maya Angelou

Olivia's week with her children was uninterrupted. She was able to divert all of her messages for the entire week. They were actively engaged from the very first day. On the last day, Isabella insisted on hiring a photographer for a family photoshoot on the beach. She persuaded everyone wear all-white attire and that each of them include three completely different wardrobes. Olivia laughed as she remembered shopping on the day before the scheduled photoshoot. She and Isaiah were finished three hours before Isabella even entered a dressing room.

Olivia also remembered them being too exhausted to even think about patronizing a restaurant, so they ordered takeout and slept as if they had been volunteering all day in extreme heat building a Habitat for Humanity home. Once everyone was up and lounging around, Isabella came up with the idea of a spa day. Isaiah went ballistic and wanted no more to do with any of it, including a family portrait. Somehow, Isabella convinced him otherwise. Olivia was so glad that her spa had some cancellations. Later, Isaiah admitted that he enjoyed himself and had the nerve to schedule another appointment for a full-body massage for next month's visit home.

Olivia was now looking at the portrait in her living area and continued to smile as she remembered the morning of the shoot. The shoot was scheduled for 9:00 a.m.; even though everyone agreed on the time, Olivia knew her children's mornings always began at noon. Olivia had gotten up at 5:00 a.m. for her morning routine with her trainer and even cooked a full breakfast. Needless to say, they ate breakfast at noon. Fortunately, the photographer had another cancellation and was able to rearrange his schedule.

Olivia glanced at all the portraits strategically placed throughout her condo. She loved them all. She missed her children when they were gone, but she was comforted in knowing that they would be back next month for a long Labor Day weekend. Olivia glanced at her wall clock and was relieved that she had decided to take Monday off. She was exhausted from everything, especially her exercise regimen. Now, if she went even one day without working out, her body ached, but she was enjoying the fruit of her labor.

A knock at the door broke Olivia's thoughts. She knew she had an hour to relax before she was scheduled to meet with her trainer, but they were supposed to meet in the gym downstairs. Security was tight in her building, and no one had called from the front desk to alert her of any possible guests.

Olivia hesitantly approached the door and glanced through the peephole. She could not believe it. It was Floyd. She seriously thought about not answering and wondered why he was so persistent in trying to explain to her in detail why he could not develop a relationship with her. Olivia felt like she needed to hear his story, so she opened the door but did not allow him to enter her home.

"Good morning, Olivia. I hope I am not interfering with your schedule too much," he said shyly.

Olivia was truly upset. She wondered what could be so very

important for him to come to her home unannounced and definitely uninvited. She truly thought that she would never see him again— not on purpose. This guy had never come to her home. In fact, he made it a point to tell her that he would not do anything to allude to a friendship and definitely not a possible relationship. She had never heard a man say anything like that to her. At least he was honest in such an odd manner. Olivia honestly thought he prided himself in doing so. Coming to her home was too much for her, but she wanted to hear what he had to say. At this very moment, Olivia thought he was a complete jerk.

Olivia was candid with him. "Look, what do you want?"

She made this statement with her hand on her hip. This stance was natural. Even though she had not taught middle school English in years, her students would know this posture meant she had had enough. Oliva was definitely not going to be nice to Floyd by any means.

"I understand that you may think this is odd," he stuttered.

Olivia was not going to give him any slack.

He just stood there awkwardly, but Olivia was not going to offer him entry into her home, a seat, anything to drink, and not even tap water.

He continued, "I am intrigued by you. At first I thought you were too much, and I quickly became intimidated by your strength, forwardness, and candidness. We met at a time when I needed to be alone, or I thought that I did. Now I am having second thoughts."

Olivia was speechless. She thought that she had made it clear that she was cool with the entire situation. She put up with the awkwardness during the dinner with Octavia and William. Why was he saying this now? She had actually become hooked on the notion of being alone. She had learned to adjust and was really enjoying it, now. The solace was becoming addictive. She was still amazed at how much time she had to accomplish just about everything on her daily to-do list. Now she was exploring her bucket list.

Floyd interrupted her thoughts by asking her for a date.

This took Olivia by surprise, which prompted her to speak without thinking. "Why now, Floyd? You made it perfectly clear that you did not want a relationship and made it abundantly clear that it was not going to be with me."

Floyd eagerly stated, "You have been on my mind since I saw you at church, and the dinner at your sister's home …" Floyd hesitated.

"Why now?" Olivia interrupted him.

Olivia could tell that he was scrambling for words. She wanted to go easy on him, but she did not care anymore. She knew that she was a good catch even in her late forties. She was also tired of men taking her for granted. She was not going to hang around any longer. She was not going to continue to beat a dead horse like she did with Victor. She wasted five years of life waiting for him until she made that decision to completely leave him alone. She remembered that she wanted closure; she wanted a goodbye, but she never received one.

Olivia remembered texting Victor: "Sometimes, I wanted to hope that things would change. That you would actually call me instead of texting. I feel it in my spirit that one day we will be in a respectful friendship. Right now, I am not feeling anything even though, at times, I miss you. Well, goodbye, Mr. Victor Daniel Lawrence. I hope our paths cross again, when we are both ready."

Floyd was interrupting not only her life but her thoughts. He was becoming annoying. She was actually seeing him in a different light, x-ray.

"Olivia, Olivia," Floyd said, interrupting her thoughts.

"What?" Olivia said, momentarily forgetting that he was even standing in her doorway. Months ago, she would have welcomed all of this attention but not now.

He continued, "Maybe we can just go for a walk. What are you doing now?"

Olivia was taken aback by his boldness, for she was the one who was always initiating contact. She honestly did not think he had it in him, yet she could not deny it. This whole thing was flattering.

Olivia's thoughts raced. She was enjoying her single life, but she had never experienced anyone giving her this much attention since her husband, Isaiah Sr., had passed over seven years ago. Olivia honestly felt as if Floyd's feelings and expressions were authentic, but she was afraid. The hurt that she experienced with Victor was a deeply rooted hurt. Sometimes she would find herself wanting to send a message, but she knew that it would only lead her into believing that he had changed when he had not.

Floyd interrupted Olivia's thoughts again. "So are you busy now? Maybe we can stroll on the beach and check out the new seafood restaurant. I believe it opened last weekend."

Olivia was actually going to check it out this weekend but alone.

"If you are too busy now, I can come around six thirty on Saturday. This will give us plenty of time to walk the shore and talk before our seven p.m. reservation. I took the liberty to reserve one of the private rooms overlooking the Gulf of Mexico. I cannot wait for you to view the sunset. Yes, I want to make our evening one to remember."

Olivia thought she was in a dream as she remembered the past ...

"Where are we going, Isaiah? Olivia asked. Deep down, Olivia knew where Isaiah was taking her. They had been waiting for this day. They were young. Olivia was just out of college, and Isaiah had just completed a brief assignment overseas. He was an airman for the United States Air Force. Olivia had been in bliss since their first date over two years ago. They had been engaged since December 16, 1994. Today, about two and a half years later, her only love was going to take her as his bride.

"Isaiah, what should I wear?" asked Olivia.

"It really does not matter," he said.

Olivia noticed Isaiah wearing khaki pants with a matching banded-collar, long sleeve shirt, so she decided to match him with a nice dress. The late morning was cooler than normal; it was breezy and crisp. It was what many called that Easter snap. It smelled of autumn, but to Olivia this day marked the beginning of her spring.

Olivia was reminded often of that day when she looked at her wedding dress. Of course, she was about fifty pounds lighter, but she also still had the two-piece suit she wore on the day of his funeral.

Floyd interrupted her thoughts again. "So, is seven p.m. a good time for you?"

Olivia simply stared at him. Her mood changed. She would ask God often why her husband was gone but decided to leave a Victor and a Floyd on Earth. She had learned early that she was not going to be able to find another Isaiah. In her head, she knew that she must move on, but her heart had to catch up. She tried to stay clear of distractions. When things did not work out initially with Floyd, she felt that she misunderstood and thought her infatuation was simply dividing her attention from her personal goals. But here he was in her doorway …

"Floyd, I am very busy right now. I was actually on my way to meet my trainer," Olivia said without losing her composure or stance. However, she was honestly intrigued.

"So, what about this weekend?" Floyd said eagerly.

Olivia did not want to tell him anything too quickly. "How about I contact you on Thursday evening?" She added, "I am actually headed to a conference in Texas tomorrow, but I will be back on Thursday evening."

"Yes, that would be fine, but if you need someone to take you to the airport, I would be happy to assist," Floyd added.

Olivia was in shock. This was a man who had been so candid with her and had hurt her feelings so deeply. As a widow, she recognized that once she would chance her heart to open and love fails, the hurt from her first love lost would surface. This type of pain would take weeks or months to heal. She experienced this with Victor. She could not realize it at first. She just thought it was natural for her to hurt for her late husband. After the last encounter with Victor, she recognized it and was able to deal with it. She asked God to take away all of the emotional baggage that she had ever experienced. Olivia did not even want to feel anything for anyone. Right now, Olivia felt just that. She would think of Victor, but her feelings for him had finally been resolved. She could not believe that Floyd was standing in front of her asking her for a date.

"No, thank you, for I do not need a ride." Olivia said. "I will just contact you when I get back."

"Okay," Floyd said with enthusiasm. "Have a safe trip. Maybe we will have an opportunity to talk while you are on your trip."

Olivia was still holding the door open as they spoke. A couple of people passing looked, apparently displeased at their conversation in the hallway, but Olivia was not going to allow Floyd to enter her home and especially unannounced.

Floyd hesitated as he turned to leave. Olivia also paused, not knowing what to expect next. She did not and could not see or even avoid his warm kiss and embrace. It was not sexual or alluring, but it was a simple embrace with a kiss on her right cheek. Before Olivia could say anything, even in protest, he was halfway down the hallway, yelling to her neighbors to hold the elevator.

Olivia blushed. She remembered why she was so drawn to him. It was not because of his muscular over six-foot-six physique, deep brown eyes, salt and pepper beard, or even deep, melancholy voice. It was this—the potential of this very moment.

Olivia was so mesmerized that she did not hear Victor's special ringtone. At first, Olivia thought she was hearing things, but when she finally got to the phone, the caller ID, along with his picture displayed on her iPhone screen, said it all. It was Victor.

"Heeellllo," Olivia said slowly.

"Hi, Olivia. This is Victor," Victor said. Olivia knew he was smiling, and she actually was too.

Chapter 4

. . . . ⚬⚭ . . . .

Set

My sun sets to rise again.

—Robert Browning

Olivia was preparing her personal items to leave for her trip tomorrow, and she pondered what had transpired, all within just one day. She never thought she would ever be in a position to choose.

Later that same day, Floyd showered her with a Musing@ Luxury Calla Lily Bouquet by Vera Wang. Olivia knew the price tag because each year she would lay these same flowers on her late husband's grave. Of course, Floyd delivered them personally. When she opened the door for the second time, Olivia noticed how strikingly handsome he was with his salt and pepper, freshly cut and shaved beard. She remembered how much she admired his closely tapered cut, which accented his deep wavy hair. Apparently he noticed her admiring look. Blushing, she looked away and turned her attention to the lovely arrangement of lilies.

"Thank you, Floyd," she said. "They are beautiful."

"Just like you," Floyd said with a smile.

Olivia was a little surprised. She did not want to hurt his feelings, but she needed to address his unannounced visits. Before she could say a word, he spoke.

"And yes, this will be my last unannounced break in, but I wanted to give these to you before you left. I could not trust delivery service," he added.

Olivia interrupted him by reminding him, "Our building does provide such services."

"I know, but I desired to see you again," Floyd admitted. "Olivia, I am smitten by you."

Olivia was speechless. By then, many of Olivia neighbors were either returning from work, leaving for dinner, or leaving for their evening stroll on the beach. Olivia had actually planned an evening of journaling before retreating to her jacuzzi because she was still tired after her session with her trainer. He made sure she endured an intense workout after discovering that Olivia had gained five pounds over the course of her vacation week with her children. But here was Floyd in her doorway, still surprising her. Olivia thought her life was going well. She was set—at least she thought she was.

She invited Floyd inside. He immediately thanked her and asked her where he could place the flowers. She had to admit that they were simply beautiful. She directed him to the kitchen, where he placed them on the counter. She then invited him to sit on the lanai. This was her best part of the day. The sun was beginning to set, and the sun's rays were dancing on the ocean's waves.

"Olivia, this is simply breathtaking," Floyd admitted.

"It is," Olivia added.

They both were mesmerized as the waves echoed all the way up to her balcony. Then she noticed that Floyd had turned his attention from the sea to her and said, "Yes, simply breathtaking."

Olivia offered Floyd a seat. All of her patio furniture faced the ocean, but somehow, Floyd still managed to position himself to gaze at her. Before she could even try to protest, he spoke.

"Oliva, would you like to grab dinner?" he asked. "I noticed when I was walking through the lobby, the restaurant special is southern cuisine this evening.

This was a great deal for Olivia to process, for she had not been pursued in this manner in years. Victor had definitely made it clear in his actions that he was the one who was typically chased in the relationship. With Victor, it never got to that level of an actual relationship. Olivia admitted that she had squandered so much of her time with Victor. Even though she hoped for a change with him, it never came. Even after she and Victor's conversation today, her feelings for him were not what they were before. Olivia knew that she was not the type of woman who needed anything from a man, for she had adjusted to living without attention from anyone. Yet Olivia was intrigued by Floyd's candid approach.

"So would you like to try their menu this evening?" he asked. "My cousin is always raving about their southern fried pork chops and homemade buttermilk biscuits. I know that you are mindful of what you consume, so I was thinking that we could simply take a stroll on the beach after dinner."

Olivia actually forgot that she had not eaten since breakfast, so she was quite famished. She thought about it. Why not? It was not like she had anything planned, and besides, she wanted to see what Floyd was all about. Their paths before had apparently crossed at a time when neither one of them were ready. Maybe now they could actually develop a friendship. But did she even need or even want a friendship with him. She could not even remember what it felt like to have emotional feelings for a man. But one thing she did know was that she was not going to even entertain the thought of marriage.

"Okay," Olivia finally pronounced.

Olivia thought Floyd was going to jump from the balcony of her lanai at that point. He soared from the lounge chair. After realizing his display of excitement, he settled back down. This made Olivia even more intrigued.

"Girl, I have met the one!"

32

Olivia could not wait to get back to her dorm room to tell all of her suitemates about Isaiah. Olivia was a senior and was just about to complete her undergraduate degree in English and political science. She was employed at a local grocery store. Isaiah happened to be one of her customers today. She was immediately drawn to his charisma. She had not actually met anyone quite like him. Immediately, she could tell that he was serious and of course, quite charming, but he was not alone. When it was his time to check out, she tried to maintain her composure. She learned later that the guy who was with him was his cousin. To this day, Olivia believed the two of them flipped a coin to see who was going to win the option of trying to talk to her. Even if his cousin had won the toss, someone spotted him and lured him into a conversation away from the checkout register. She was hoping Isaiah would ask for her phone number, and he did.

"Okay, Olivia?" Floyd said, interrupting her thoughts.

Olivia responded, "Why don't I meet you downstairs in about fifteen minutes?"

"Okay. I made reservations earlier in hopes you would agree," Floyd said, smiling.

Olivia thought he was handsome. She was actually seeing him in a different light. She definitely had not expected any of this from him.

Olivia remembered vaguely not receiving special gifts from her father or stepfather as a child; however, she still held memories of her late grandfather, who had adorned her with many gifts, in her heart. Isaiah continued where her grandfather left off. He introduced her to what it felt like to be loved and admired. He never expected anything in return, even though Olivia prided herself on being able to take care of herself. Eventually Olivia accepted his love and adoration without the feelings of guilt or expectancy.

Floyd and Victor had similar characteristics, but neither came close; however, Floyd …

Olivia was again lost in her thoughts. Olivia did not want to mislead Floyd in anyway, so she made herself a mental note to express her concerns over dinner.

"Olivia, what would you like for me to order?" he asked.

She did not want him to know she had not heard a word he was saying, so she replied, "Whatever you are having is good with me."

Again, he was grinning and showing all thirty-twos! Olivia was somewhat taken aback because he was not afraid of showing his emotions. She definitely admired that character trait.

Olivia walked Floyd to the door, and this time he left with only a smile. She could not believe she was blushing. Once she closed the door, her phone played a tone. It was Victor. She debated on answering it. Their morning conversation had been limited. He said he would call later, but this surprised her. He was keeping his word. Victor had a track record for leaving her to wonder. Sometimes she and Victor would engage in a texting conversation, and then suddenly, he would just stop texting. Earlier in their so-called friendship, Olivia would worry about his well-being, but later she learned he was just insolent. She hesitated but then answered.

"Hello," Olivia said, smiling. She was beginning to question her sanity. Why or even how could she have feelings for two guys simultaneously? Never in her forty something years had she dared to even look at a man if she was courting another one. Besides, she knew she needed to stay focus on her business trip. Olivia would be one of the keynote speakers, and she would be discussing the very principle on which her agency was founded. She would emphasize how parents play the point guard in their children's lives both on and off the court.

"Jay, are you there?" Victor asked.

Olivia loved it when he called her Jay. "Yes, I am here." Olivia said. "What's up?"

"Well, I know you are scheduled for a business trip later this week, but I was wondering if you wanted to check out that new restaurant in the strip mall along the shore tomorrow night?" asked Victor.

At this point, Olivia was looking around for cameras. She had always wanted to be an actress, but apparently *Candid Camera* would be her debut. This was surreal, almost dreamlike, but Olivia knew she was wide awake.

"Well, I was thinking we could stroll the beach to and from the restaurant," Victor suggested.

Floyd knew exactly where Olivia lived, but Victor only knew the address. Even though Victor seldom responded to any of her messages, Olivia always made it a point to inform Victor of her life events. Apparently he had researched the area. There was no way they were going to the new restaurant, but as with Floyd, Olivia was intrigued with Victor as well. Since the very beginning, Victor had always kept her at a distance. After many years, Victor had never invited Olivia into his home. She was invited to come and talk in the driveway once, but he never invited her inside. He had never really invited her into his life, for there had always been a wall between them. It was almost like a shield. No matter how much or how often Olivia revealed to him how much she cared for him and loved every part of who he was, his past, and his future, Victor never completely allowed her in. And now, he was finally here, or was he?

Olivia wanted to see if he was actually ready to allow her into every room of his total existence, so she agreed to a date.

"Since you are an impeccable chef, I suggest you cook our meal," Olivia shared.

"Okay," he agreed. "I have been wanting to try this new salmon recipe."

Olivia was mindful of the time. Floyd was waiting downstairs, but she also wanted to feel Victor out. Was he being truthful with her? Why now? "Look, I am about to grab something to eat. So, is it okay if I call you later this evening?" Olivia asked.

Olivia actually felt liberated. She and Victor's verbal conversations were limited. Well, to be truthful, they were nonexistent, no matter how much Olivia would hope otherwise.

"Okay," Victor said. "But Jay, can you at least consider having dinner with me?"

"I have," Olivia stated shyly. "However, my flight leaves in the morning, but you are allowed to make reservations for us." Olivia knew she was flirting, but this was familiarities. Even though she knew of the possible end result, she still wanted to hope for a different outcome.

"Okay. Where? Your place or mine?" Victor asked. "But I was under the impression that you were leaving the day after tomorrow."

Wow, Olivia thought. Why was he so concerned now? Were the tables finally turning? Was he going to actually pursue her?

"My flight was actually changed due to the possible threat of a tropical storm or hurricane." Olivia was pressed for time, so she continued, "Since you are the chef, let's have dinner at your place."

There was silence.

Olivia finally spoke. "I really need to go now. I will call you later."

Victor hesitantly said, "Okay, I look forward to hearing from you tonight, Jay. Maybe I can take you to the airport."

Olivia noticed the sincerity in Victor's voice. She was touched. Could she really believe that things would work out this time?

Olivia really did not want to lead Victor into even thinking he had a chance. She honestly wanted him to pursue her, but she also did not want to play any games.

"I will let you know tonight. My schedule is hectic now," she answered. She wondered if he was feeling the same way she did, for this would be his excuse so many times she wanted to see him. He was always busy.

"Okay, I hope to hear from you tonight," he finally said.

Olivia heard a little desperation in his response. She was flattered, but she also knew that she was not going to call him tonight. She had already made up in her mind that she would never pursue another man, and that meant that she would never text, call, or plan a chance meeting. She would never place herself in that vulnerable position again. The responses from both Victor and Floyd always seemed unappreciative to her.

They exchanged goodbyes, and Olivia quickly made herself presentable for an evening with Floyd. She knew some men and even some women who dated multiple people even on one given evening, but she had always prided herself on not being one of those individuals. Things were moving so swiftly that she did not even take the time to even pray for direction. She was just caught up in the moment of her feelings. For the first time in a long time, men were actually giving her more attention than she wanted.

Once Olivia arrived downstairs, she spotted Floyd immediately. Olivia thought that he was always handsome, but this time, his actions made him look more attractive. It was just so hard to believe that Floyd was being so nice and sensitive to her desires that she had forgotten she had ever wanted. She was simply in awe. The main advantage that Floyd had over Victor was his sensitive nature. Victor had never given her a thing that he actually had to spend money on. She did remember once when they were setting a date. He agreed to purchase the liquor, but at the last minute, he asked Olivia to, for he said that he would be late. Olivia had refused. Olivia had always been disappointed in Victor. She still could not figure out why she wasted so much of her time on him.

"Olivia," Floyd said, catching her attention. She had not even noticed his cologne earlier, but now with him being in arm's distance, she recognized the scent. It was the same scent of Victor's, Clive Christian C.

Floyd continued speaking as he led Olivia to her seat. "Have you ever gotten a chance to sit down here for a meal and watch the sun set?"

"No I normally order in and would just have dinner from my lanai," Olivia answered.

"But don't you think having someone to share the meal and sunset regularly would be even nicer?" he asked.

Olivia ignored his statement and quickly changed the subject by picking up the menu and suggesting various main dishes. She was embarrassed and quite flattered, for Olivia had never even imagined herself in a relationship.

She had forgotten that she told him to order for her.

After only two weeks of dating, Isaiah was expressing his feelings and was attempting to ask Olivia for a committed relationship. Olivia was ecstatic, for only one guy had ever asked her to be his woman since tenth grade, but then, that relationship only lasted for about six weeks.

"But Isaiah, what are you trying to say?" Olivia asked, giggling and blushing.

"I thought we were seeing eye to eye," Isaiah said, trying to explain.

"But did you ask me anything," Olivia was somewhat leading Isaiah into a more formal way of asking her to be his girlfriend.

"Okay, will you be my girlfriend?" Isaiah finally asked. "I am ready to settle down, and I want to be with you. I have been with many others. Women are constantly trying to snatch my attention, but I want to be in a committed relationship with you.

Not only was Olivia flattered, but she was also scared. She had only fantasized about a relationship, and in her dream, she was a caring and sensitive girlfriend. At twenty-one, and a senior at the University of Southwestern Mississippi, she had not dreamt of meeting the love of her life only two months before her graduation.

"Okay, Olivia," Floyd admitted. "Maybe I am moving too fast for you, but I know what I want now. I honestly feel that the timing has never been perfect."

Olivia thought that maybe for him, but she apparently had some decision making to do. Olivia was not sure if Victor would be an option, but she wanted to make the right decision with anyone she allowed close to her. She had been hurt before. Some hurt she had brought on herself, but the deepest hurt she had ever experienced was losing her best friend. She never thought she would ever be in the position she was in now, for every man she had encountered did not have a clue who he was or what he wanted or even deserved. Olivia was determined not to allow anyone or anything to divide her attention, for she honestly thought her future was set or established. She was actually quite content with her decision to be alone.

Floyd told her that he wanted to wait to order the meal together, and they did. After she and Floyd finally decided to both have smothered fried chicken with brown rice, cabbage, sweet potatoes with homemade dinner biscuits, and peach cobbler with vanilla ice cream, Olivia excused herself to the ladies' room. Before she could even reach the door, Victor texted.

"Olivia, I am honestly sorry for our unsteady past; however, the only thing that I will not apologize for is meeting you."

Olivia's heart sank. For months, she had been waiting on Victor to show her how much he cared and now, this …

Victor continued to text. "I am asking you for a chance to show you how much you have always meant to me. I have been afraid of rejection for so long, but now, I would rather chance rejection than to ever lose you again. I want you in my life. I am looking forward to talking with you later this evening. Tiger."

Olivia was speechless. First of all, she could not believe she had butterflies. She actually gave him his nickname, Tiger, just as he had given her hers, Jay. Why was all of this happening so soon and right now? Olivia did not respond to Victor's message because she honestly did not know what to say.

When Olivia returned, Floyd immediately helped her with her seat. She felt as if she were in the fairytale, Cinderella, but this time, the likely prince knew her. Once she was seated, Floyd smiled and Olivia followed. No matter how hard she tried not to blush, she felt her face grow warm.

"So, tell me about your upcoming business trip," Floyd said with ease.

She had always admired his charismatic style. He had a way of making you feel at ease. He had a way of making you feel comfortable. His charm was captivating. Maybe that was why she did not mind when he reached over for her hand, and she allowed the brief connection before they were served. After the food was placed strategically on their table, he again reached for her hand, but this time he grabbed both hands and prayed.

Their dialogue was in sync; they had more commonalities than she thought. Both of them commented on the food, and Floyd insisted on taking care of the bill and gratuity. This, too, was something she was not used to. Olivia exhaled and relaxed even more.

After dinner, they strolled along the beach, taking in the remaining shadows of rays from the sunset. He held her hand, and she allowed him to. Even though she wanted to walk further, he told her it was getting late. He promised her even a better evening this weekend, if she agreed to a more formal date. He did not even give her time to agree or protest before he led them back to her condo. This time he challenged her to a footrace. They both took off their shoes and raced like teenagers. She knew Floyd allowed her to win, but she did not mind doing her victory dance at their makeshift finish line. Many patrons looked on admiringly. Olivia knew that she had not had this much excitement in a very long time.

Once they were back at her door, Olivia was admittedly tired, but she knew that she and Floyd could have talked all night, and she actually wanted to talk more. Once Olivia opened the door to her home, Floyd grabbed both of her hands and leaned in. Olivia wanted to kiss him, but she knew that it was moving too quickly. She wanted to feel his warmth in more ways than she was willing to admit even to herself. Olivia closed her eyes, and Floyd raised both of her hands and kissed them both.

She opened her eyes to hear him whisper in her ear, "In due season ... get ready, set ..."

Before Olivia could even inquire about anything, Floyd was halfway up the hall, headed to the elevator. Right before the elevator door closed, he winked.

Olivia thought she was set—that her future of being single had been established. Before she heard from either Floyd or Victor, she admitted that she was content, but both men were fascinating her. She was relieved her business trip was scheduled for this week, for she needed time to process it all. She needed to hear from the Lord.

She looked at her phone, for she knew Victor would be waiting to hear from her. She opted not to call him, not because she still remembered the many phone calls he never returned or the text messages that went unanswered, but because she honestly did not know who or what she wanted at this point. All she wanted to do was focus on things she could control. That was one of the reasons why her business was thriving; Olivia also took solace in working. This was how she had been coping since Isaiah passed. She had learned early that he could not be replaced. The feelings and emotions had to be resolved. She knew this was why she and Victor were never quite compatible. No matter what happened, they actually really did not sync. Olivia was not sure if she ever wanted to go down that path again, not just with Victor but with Floyd either. She was actually in a better place mentally, emotionally, spiritually, and physically. She knew God was her divine healer, so going back to either man might be like going back to a place of hurt. She now understood that experiencing hurt when you have not resolved your feelings with previous relationships would not only stop your healing process but would take you back. One could even experience that same level of hurt and sometimes even on a greater scale. Olivia was happy she was going out of town in the morning. She needed to gather her thoughts. She needed direction.

Olivia silenced her phone and retreated to her oversized jetted whirlpool tub. She dropped in a couple of bath bombs, got in, and closed her eyes. She knew that whatever happened, she would be set because she refused to allow her emotions to cloud her sound judgment. It took her years to finally break free of her emotions with Victor, and they had never been in a committed relationship. She had not been in any type of relationship since her Isaiah passed. There was no way she was going to tarnish his memory by allowing any and everything in her personal space. No one had yet qualified. It seemed as if perhaps no one ever would.

Chapter 5

Diversion

Rushing around can be a pointless diversion from
actually living your life.

—Claire Messud

Olivia woke up the next morning reinvigorated, for she was
ready to divert all of the distractions into something that
mattered. She enjoyed running her nonprofit agency and embraced
any opportunity for a reprieve or diversion from her current situation.

Olivia was able to get in a thirty-minute workout before her
scheduled flight. Although she loved her trainer, she enjoyed the
opportunity to exercise without any distractions. She was even able
to listen to one of her favorite television ministers. Olivia called all
of her family members to confirm their plans for her stepfather's
surprise birthday party, and she was heading out the door when
she received a text simultaneously from both Floyd and Victor. She
did not respond to either of them. Olivia paused as she was leaving,
thinking that she had forgotten her keys. She remembered that she
had placed them on her kitchen counter. She retrieved them and
glanced at the flowers, which were right where Floyd had placed

them. She had not really given much thought to the flowers or who had given them to her this morning, and she still had no clue who grave her the previous bouquet of roses. She wanted to place all of it in the back of her mind until she returned from her business trip. She noticed another message from her sister, whom she had been avoiding since the Sunday dinner show featuring the main character, Floyd. Olivia made a mental note to call her sister once she settled into her hotel room later that evening. She sent Octavia a greeting and a promise to call her once she was settled.

The flight was smooth and uneventful. Olivia was able to respond to all of her emails and worked on the next fiscal year's budget. Even though Olivia had the best grant writers and accountants, she always chose to see firsthand all of the business expenditures. It did not help that she avoided any forms of math or statistic classes in undergraduate school and graduate school. She admitted that this department was a struggle for her but delegating was not an option for her; she had known many people to lose not only their nonprofit agency but their personal assets as a result of placing too much trust in individuals. After reviewing the figures for about two hours, Olivia decided that the numbers were good. She did need a distraction from everything, but tonight, she felt as if she needed to finally return Victor's phone call. She could remember a time when he never was in any hurry to respond to anything she ever had to say. He did not call her, nor did he accept her calls most of the time, so practically all of their conversations were initiated by her.

"So are we going to hang out this weekend?" Olivia would text.

"I am not sure. I have to work," he would answer.

Each time she would send a text, she would always promise to herself that it would be her last. She and Victor would go days and weeks without ever seeing each other, but she would always hope that one day they would actually go on a date. She would always send suggestions, but most of the time, those suggestions would not receive a response. She knew that she needed to break the cycle. It took her years of ups and downs and highs and lows, but she finally was able to be consistent in not contacting him.

"Dr. Bentley ... Dr. Bentley?" the neighboring passenger said, calling her name. "They asked us to buckle up for landing."

"Yes, thank you. I was wrapped up in my thoughts," Olivia responded.

"Si, I understand, senorita, but safety first." she added. "By the way, I am Maria Isabella Garcia."

Olivia remembered that they had expressed pleasantries but had not formally exchanged greetings.

"Were you able to finish all of your reports?" Maria asked.

"Si, Senorita Maria," Olivia replied.

Olivia was grateful that she and her sister had decided to study abroad for a year. Being able to speak fluent Spanish as well as a little French definitely helped with the amount of traveling she does. She and Maria continued the rest of their conversation in Spanish. They made plans to meet the next morning for breakfast; fortunately, they were staying at the same five-star hotel, which was actually where the conference was held this year. Maria was the cofounder of a battered women's shelter. Their doors only opened a few months ago, and Olivia was always eager to share or help anyone with every detail of running a nonprofit. In fact, Olivia was seriously considering adding a women's shelter as well as a day care for the elderly.

She and Maria shared a cab and chatted about everything. Olivia was surprised at their commonalities; however, Maria had been divorced for two years. Olivia was grateful for any distractions because she needed and wanted to avoid thinking about either man. It was noon, so she was eager to get settled into her hotel room. She wanted to review her financial report a final time before submitting the report to the state in the morning. Besides, she needed to make contact with her business manager before she was satisfied with the numbers. William Bryant, J's Next Generations of Youth 2415 business manager, had graduated top of his class in business law. He was young and full of more ideas than Olivia could keep track of. Olivia admired his spontaneity, and she hoped someday she could trust him with more responsibility. But right now, he was learning. Olivia knew that William had better offers, so she knew how fortunate she was to have him on her team. She was able to provide him a base salary of $250,000, which was, of course, nothing compared to his net worth.

Olivia reviewed the numbers again, called William, and then took a relaxing bath. Olivia realized she missed her children and called them as well. Both were available to talk. Of course, Isaiah II was brief, but Isabella's conversation took an hour. Olivia also called her sister; however, Octavia made her promise lunch as soon as she returned.

Olivia ordered room service, and as soon as she was settled into bed, Victor called. She was hoping to also corner him into a brief conversation. She held her breath and answered. Before Olivia even spoke, Victor began asking multiple questions without waiting for her to respond. Olivia was in total shock. Never had she seen this side of him, so caring and concerned about her well-being.

"So are you coming tonight?" Olivia asked. This was, she felt, her hundredth text message, but Olivia was excited. She and Victor had met for lunch earlier that day, and he was thinking about coming over later that night. Olivia had suggested games and was looking forward to getting to know Victor. She was ready to talk all night.

"I am not sure; one of my vehicles needs servicing. Besides, Olivia, I am not sure if we are compatible," Victor finally said.

Olivia could not believe it. She thought their conversations were in sync. She simply could not believe that she was not going to see him tonight. No doubt Olivia knew she could be intense and maybe even demanding. Her expectancy levels were high because of what she had experienced with Isaiah. His death made her reevaluate what was important. She knew she was in love with Victor when she first met him, but she had no clue about the dating scene and the multiple games men played well into their adult years. She learned men played games mainly because of fear—the fear of being "whipped" by a woman he was in love with.

"Olivia, are you there?" Victor asked.

"Yes. And yes, the flight was uneventful," she answered the only question she remembered hearing.

"Great! Sorry about all of the questions, but I was worried when you did not call last night or answer my text," he added.

Why did Victor feel as if he had the liberty to ask her anything? For the past year, Olivia had no one, other than her family, who cared enough to ask her anything. Olivia did learn quickly the drastic responsibilities of being a single mother, but she always had this notion that one day Isaiah would return. She wanted to believe he would defy the laws of death, even after being buried.

"Yes, Victor, all is well and thanks for being concerned, but I travel alone all the time," Olivia reassured him. However, she was wondering why she was reassuring him of anything.

"Well, maybe we can start travelling together," he stated with calmness and confidence.

Olivia was taken aback by his statement.

"Let's meet at Beach Park at 8:30 p.m.," Victor texted.

"Okay," Oliva responded.

Olivia was so happy. Even though she had settled in for the night, she got out of bed and redressed. She was going to finally see Victor. After months of his excuses and her indecisiveness, they were finally meeting. Olivia did not want to admit that they were only meeting and not actually going on a date. She had promised him a gift, and he was simply meeting with her to retrieve it. Olivia knew that this was outside of her character, but she would at times do anything to get his attention. Olivia refused to admit that he did not want her as a girlfriend. He acted like he had no respect for her; she had no respect for herself at times.

Ignoring his statement, Olivia responded with a giggle. It was not a flirtatious giggle, but it was simply a giggle she did not even care how he interpreted.

He chuckled and said, "I miss your laugh."

This was strange because Olivia felt that their lack of phone conversation was because he disliked her laugh and her voice.

Victor continued, "I know that you are probably tired, but I only wanted to hear your voice. I wanted to make sure you were safe. The forecast is predicting a tropical storm heading to Texas in a couple of days, but I hope it does not strengthen into a hurricane."

Olivia was well aware of the possibility of a storm, but she was hoping the weather would not deteriorate while she was still in Houston.

Olivia wanted to suddenly end the conversation. She could not believe that all of a sudden Victor was showing her signs that he was a human being. She was becoming literally nauseated. She did not know why. She had noticed during their last conversation that her stomach became upset, but she concluded it was something she had eaten. Maybe she had jet lag, but she was very nauseated now.

Room service knocked on her door. Maybe that was it; she immediately remembered she had not had anything to eat for hours. Maybe the nauseous sensation was due to hunger.

Victor must have heard someone at the door. He said, "I guess your meal has arrived, so I guess we can continue this conversation later. I am going to say good night, and I am looking forward to your return. I am ready to be your chef." Before Olivia could question him, he said, "Yes, Jay, dinner at my house. I will be your chef for an evening and maybe for evenings to come.

"Again, good night, Dr. Jay, and sweet dreams."

Olivia simply responded, "Good night."

Olivia did not know exactly why, but she was eager to end the conversation Victor. She remembered feeling a little nauseated during their interactions, but now the sensation to vomit subsided. It was somewhat questionable because she still had not eaten yet.

Olivia decided not to entertain those thoughts for now; she was famished. She walked to her hotel door and allowed the hotel's food service to enter.

Olivia devoured everything. She had ordered lemon dill salmon with garlic, white wine, and butter sauce with rice and steamed green beans. She replaced her bread and slice of cake with a frozen chocolate custard with walnuts, drizzled with chocolate syrup, and she had two bottles of water.

Feeling a little guilty after her meal, Olivia decided to go for a walk. Once she was outside, she noticed a light breeze coming from the south. She remembered Victor mentioning the forecast for the Houston area, but right now, the sunset was breathtaking. She increased the volume to her favorite playlist and tried to match her strides with the beat. Houston was a beautiful place even though Olivia, admittedly, had never wanted to reside in a state with sweltering heat during the intense summer months. She remembered plenty of family reunions, road trips, and being stranded on the interstate in impassible traffic. She could not even fathom the daily commute.

As Olivia was strolling by local restaurants, for some reason, she made direct eye contact with someone through one window. She was not even sure how it happened, but the glance was somewhat intense. He smiled, and with a natural response, she reciprocated the smile. Olivia was distracted by the vibration of her phone. She broke her glance and saw that it was Floyd. When she looked up again, the stranger in the window was intently engaged in what apparently looked like a business meeting. Olivia was quite familiar with dinner meetings, some that would last until closing hours. Olivia responded to Floyd's message. Olivia was more at ease with Floyd than Victor. However, she could not pinpoint exactly why. She had promised to phone him in the morning before her conferences began. It was getting too late, and she did not feel like speaking with anyone now. She turned around and headed back to the hotel when she spotted him again. This time he and his apparent business associates were outside of the restaurant. She could feel his eyes follow her, but she refused to look in his direction. As a diversion, Olivia noticed a different path, which led to her hotel. She took it and never even glanced back.

Once inside the hotel, Olivia spotted Maria, who was sitting at the bar speaking with a few individuals. And of course, she was speaking Texas's second language, Spanish. Maria spotted Olivia and excused herself.

"Si, Olivia," she said. "I see you have been becoming familiar with the area."

"Houston is simply breathtaking," Olivia responded.

"It is!" she added. "I was networking, and we are actually arranging a tour of the city tomorrow after the conference."

"Count me in," Olivia exclaimed. "I was able to get just a taste of the city as I was strolling." Olivia had to admit her enthusiasm was in part due to the man who had caught her eye earlier.

Olivia paused. Here she was in Houston acting like a teenager. Her main goal was to minimize distractions, and here she stood in a cloud of uncertainty. Why was she allowing herself to be distracted? She was doing all of the right things. She was confident in keeping her spirit, mind, soul, and body under subjection, under control.

Maria continued, "Well, I will review the details with you in the morning during breakfast. I am going to check out the custard shop that everyone has been raving about."

"Yes, it was my dessert, and that is why I had to take a stroll this evening. It was delicious calories!" Olivia added. "Well, I will meet you in the morning around seven fifteen a.m."

"Great," Maria said. They exchanged hugs, and Maria rejoined her group.

Just as Olivia was making her way to the elevator, she saw him. She could not believe it. She again made herself scarce, as she quickly moved into the elevator. As the doors were closing, they exchanged glances. There was no way that he could have made his way to the elevator before the doors closed. Olivia was relieved yet disappointed. She did not know why she was disappointed, but she was.

Once she was finally settled in for the night, someone knocked on the door. By this time, Olivia was really tired. It was around 8:30, and the jet lag was finally taking its toll.

"Delivery from the front desk," a young man's voice called out.

Reluctantly, Olivia grabbed a jacket, because she could not find the robe she had packed, and opened the door.

"Sorry, ma'am, I did not know you had already settled in for the night," the young man said.

Olivia was not sure about her appearance, but the young man seem to be accustomed to this. Olivia had even forgotten she had washed her hair that evening and was wearing a scarf tightly around her head. At that moment, she remembered that she was too tired to completely dry her hair, for it was a little damp.

The young man broke her thoughts. "A Maria wanted you to have this tonight.

Taking the note, Olivia was confused, for she wondered why Maria could not have just called her or waited to speak with her in the morning.

Olivia was able to grab her purse to retrieve a few bills and thank the messenger. She closed and locked the door. Even though she was tired, she opted not to place the note on the night stand to read it in the morning. Apparently, it must be important, so she turned on the light as she sat in the bed and read.

"Hi, I hope this is not too forward, but I saw you three times in one evening. Numbers have symbolic meaning. Anyway, I asked Maria to send you this note. I have known Maria for a little over a year now. I attempted to get your attention all three times this evening but was unsuccessful. Since Maria is quite social, I asked her about you. Even though she was hesitant, she promised that she would get this note to you. I do hope you are reading it. Yes, we both saw you disappear to the elevator in record time."

Olivia laughed aloud and continued reading. "I do hope we have an opportunity to formally meet, and by the way, I'm Alexander Hamilton Carrington, and I guess you are Dr. J? Maria did not share your full name. Well, until tomorrow, good night."

Olivia was wide awake.

Chapter 6

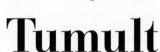

Tumult

Challenges make you discover things about yourself
that you never really knew.

—Cicely Tyson

O livia could not remember ever receiving this much attention.
For months, she had been diligent in areas of her life that
actually mattered. She was maintaining her focus on her family, her
business, and even her friends. Discovering a mate or being depressed
by not having a relationship had lain dormant; she purposely ignored
anyone who showed the slightest interested. Now it looked as if
Olivia had been bombarded by three men.

Olivia was able to speak briefly with her best friend, Ava, last
night before dozing off around ten p.m. Ava could not believe what
had transpired since their last conversation about two weeks ago. Ava
and Olivia had been friends for years. They met when Olivia was
working as a service-learning coordinator at the same university Ava
was attending. In spite of the age difference, they had maintained a
close friendship. Together, they had experienced divorces, marriages,

childbirths, and the passing of Isaiah. Olivia remembered when they decided to become business partners.

"Let's have a working dinner. Besides, I have been craving pizza *all* day," Olivia exclaimed.

Olivia was pregnant with Isabella and had been experiencing the most bizarre food cravings as well as wanting inedible items, such as red clay dirt and Charmin ultra-soft. It definitely did not help that a contracting company was building a duplex apartment right behind there home; she could simply walk out their back door and get as much as she wanted. One of her neighbors suggested that she bake it, but Olivia refused.

"Girl, you and your cravings," Ava responded.

"Girl, yes, this pregnancy is a little different from Isaiah II," Olivia added.

In the midst of their girl talk at the dining room table, Isaiah entered the kitchen.

He said sarcastically, "I thought you ladies were working." He came over and kissed Olivia on the forehead and then asked if the pizza had arrived. Isaiah II was behind him.

"Hi! Ms. Ava. Mom, I am hungry," Isaiah added.

"Deuce, I told you about formally speaking," his father added.

"Sorry," Deuce replied. He then turned to Ava, shook her hand, and added, "Good evening, Ms. Ava Davison. How are you doing?"

Olivia could tell that Ava was shocked and said later that they were definitely doing a great job in raising Deuce. She also said that she did not know of many three-year-olds who could hold a conversation with any adult. Olivia knew that was the highest reason for her attraction to her husband. His mannerisms were of the highest of anyone whom she had ever met.

Before Isaiah and Deuce went back to their man cave, Ava asked Isaiah if he had any specifics that he wanted to include in the grant proposal in reference to his sports section.

"Focus on getting the agency up and running," Isaiah said. As he and Deuce were leaving the room, he added, "And call us when the pizza arrives."

Olivia tried to ask Isaiah a few specifics, but he simply turned around and blew her a kiss.

Ava continued, "I am not believing my ears. Three men are chasing you."

Olivia laughed because she remembered just a few months ago how she was dreading attending her agency's Christmas party again dateless, but now she had the possibility of choice.

"Right," Olivia said, laughing and speaking simultaneously. She remembered how Victor would mock her laugh. She still wondered if her laugh and voice were the reasons why they seldom communicated.

"So please, tell me you will be seeing Alexander, tomorrow after your conference?" Ava asked.

"Girl, he frightens me," Olivia admitted.

"Seriously?" asked Ava. Not waiting on a response, she added, "I have heard your stories of how you met Isaiah."

"But this is different. This is a different time. I honestly have not ever heard a love story quite like me and Isaiah's. Only Floyd has ever come close, and you see what happened with that," Olivia said.

"I wish you would not be a pessimist, Olivia. Love is out there waiting for you to find," Ava said.

"No, ma'am. Love will have to find *me*, now. Look at my history," Olivia said.

"True, but you have to allow it to happen," Ava finally said.

Olivia knew this to be true, but she was having issues with the men who were resurfacing.

Olivia and Ava ended their conversation with prayer, and Olivia retreated into preparing her presentation for the conference and then had a peaceful night's sleep.

Olivia woke energized, refreshed, and ready for her presentation. This would be her first time to deliver her message, her passion for creating J's Next Generation of Youth 2415. It was estimated that over fifteen hundred attendees would be present for the conference's opening session. She was also invited to speak at a number of breakout sessions. Olivia was delighted to publicly speak, for this was the opportunity she had been anticipating for years. She smiled when she thought about how far she had come. She knew that without her faith she would be lost. She smiled as she pondered where God had brought her. It was not her financial wealth or even her agency; it was her peace of mind for which she was most grateful. Olivia was so wrapped up in her thoughts that she lost track of time. She glanced at her phone. There was a "good morning" from Victor and a missed call from Floyd. She remembered how she would anxiously wait for any response from Victor. She also remembered the disappointment at not receiving a reply at all.

Olivia again felt nauseous. She opted not to respond to Victor's message but returned Floyd's call. She had about fifteen minutes to spare before she met Maria for breakfast.

Olivia smiled. She could not figure out why she was smiling at the thought of Floyd. Maybe it was because he was honest with her, unlike Victor, who she discovered had a number of women he juggled. Floyd was focused on his career and family. Olivia realized now that she should have respected him, if not for anything else but for his honesty, even if he did not necessarily say it in the most proper way.

Floyd answered on the first ring and spoke first.

"Hi, Olivia. I take it that all is well," he said.

Olivia could tell immediately that he was smiling. She smiled back.

"Yes, all is well. Thank God," Olivia replied. Another thing that Floyd had over Victor was his persona. Floyd had a genuineness that was captivating. Olivia felt as if she could speak freely with him.

"So, are you ready for your presentation?" Floyd asked.

"I am," Olivia said with confidence. She was surprisingly comfortable with him.

They chatted for a few more minutes before saying their goodbyes. Floyd promised to send up additional prayers for her today. He admitted to her during dinner that he prayed for her daily and sometimes when he was just thinking of her. Again, Olivia was even more intrigued. Floyd was saying and doing all the right things. But could she really trust him?

As Olivia was leaving her room, she finally decided to return Victor's "good morning." He immediately sent an emoji. She could not believe it. She recalled the days when she would have settled for an emoji when the conversations she craved did not exist. Olivia was definitely not going to send him anything in return. Olivia's stomach flipped. Maybe she was simply hungry.

Olivia finally made her way downstairs. Olivia spotted Maria first. She was, of course, networking. Olivia had hoped to have a private conversation about Alexander, but there were crowds of people. Olivia felt a little excitement but not hunger. Olivia decided to save the conversation about Alexander for later and eat after her presentation.

The convocation began promptly. Olivia was the third panelist to speak. She always came equipped with multiple slideshows to choose freebies and handouts galore, but during every presentation, her heart would always take over. Even though she knew this was not necessarily for religious-based organizations, she seemed to always allow her emotions to reveal her heart. At a conference of fifteen hundred individuals, there was probably not a dry eye in the building. Olivia was always amazed at how the Holy Spirit would capture her presentation. There were times when Olivia could not even remember what she spoke during her message, but after each presentation, she would realize even more that she never wanted to ever leave God's presence.

During lunch, Oliva had an opportunity to network as well as eat a satisfying meal. She was now beginning to see her body adjust to a proper diet, and the redeveloping curves were not bad. Olivia could now wear some of her old clothing comfortably. Olivia went through the rest of the day with ease; however, around five p.m., she was famished and a little fatigued. It was a good fatigue, and she was ready to retire for the evening. She was going to dodge the outing with Maria. She had seen Alexander earlier but was able to avoid him.

Olivia made it to her room uneventfully, but when she arrived, there was a message from the front desk. Olivia was surprised and shocked to hear that she had three packages at the front desk, which were sent to her room immediately. Olivia opened the door at the first knock of her hotel to discover that she was receiving a single rose from Alexander, Floyd, and Victor. This was way too much. She opted not to respond to them immediately. At this point, she wanted to eat, work out, and take a nap, or maybe she was in a dream. She definitely did not want to risk seeing Alexander, because she did not know if he was actually staying at the hotel. Apparently he had figured out her identity. She was indeed flattered by all of the attention, but she thought she was losing focus. She remembered a number of her friends encouraging her to date, but Olivia was never one to have multiple anything. However, under the circumstances, it might be a good idea. Olivia knew she had no intentions of marriage, and both Victor and Floyd's first impressions were not anything to display in a trophy case. And this Alexander …

Olivia's thoughts were interrupted by five incoming text messages. She merely glanced at them. Two were from Victor, one from Floyd, one from Maria, and one from Alexander. She read Alexander's. Apparently, Marie had given Alexander her contact information.

"Olivia, please forgive me again for being forward, but I would love to meet you for dinner or coffee later. Please do not be upset with Marie, for I am an excellent persuader! Alex."

Olivia was tired. She chose sleep and set her alarm for 7 p.m.

Olivia woke two minutes before her alarmed sounded. She was refreshed but quite famished. She texted both Victor and Floyd to thank them for the rose and told them both that she would call them later this evening. Olivia knew the history of Victor's single rose, but was uncertain of Floyd's until he responded, "I will send you a rose each day until you come 'home.'" Olivia noticed the quotes around home but decided to not ponder it.

Olivia hoped that she could keep up with all of this, but she knew Victor did not have a leg to stand on. He might be the first one to go. She texted Alex to thank him and to take him up on his invite. She called Maria to tell her what was going on. Maria, of course, was too excited and admitted that she was indeed jealous but wished her well. Alex texted back, and they made plans to meet in the lobby in about thirty minutes. They decided to discuss their plans for the evening then. Olivia was glad she had decided to shower before napping. She decided to wear jeans but dressed it up with a sheer navy top with matching slides. She was uncertain about where they were going or how Alexander would dress, but Olivia was cute and comfortable.

She spotted him immediately. She was surprised at how strikingly handsome he was. She was happy to see him in jeans accompanied in a crisp, collared white long-sleeve shirt. Apparently he must have seen her admiringly stare. Olivia felt her face grow warm, and they both smiled simultaneously. He was able to break away from a group discussion and head her way. She noticed his full physique; he was about six foot four at about 225. His smile was mesmerizing.

"Hi, Dr. Benton," Alexander said with a smile. "How are you?"

Olivia tried not to smile, but she thought he was so attractive. "Hi, Alexander," she finally said. They stood there in complete silence until Olivia finally asked where they were going. Still Alexander stood there for a beat staring at her before he finally started making suggestions.

It was apparent that the attractions were mutually felt, but it had been months since Olivia had a desire to even entertain those thoughts. She was finally at a stage in her life where she no longer envied couples she would see at restaurants, at the mall, or even at the grocery store. Olivia avoided vacations because she would see families that resembled what she and her children once had. Time does not necessarily heal, but it makes it better. It had taken years for Olivia to be comfortable eating in restaurants alone, but she still avoided the movie theatre. Many of her girlfriends would tell her that she would rush with men or that she would work too hard. Maybe that was some of the feelings of guilt. She regretted not doing more for Isaiah, but it was clear that every man she would meet did not even deserve what she had to offer. She also knew that she could not settle for men with many flaws. When she would meet guys, some would feel comfortable in revealing some of their history. It always centered around an ex-wife or long-time ex-girlfriend breaking their hearts. Olivia would always feel that he would eventually rekindle that relationship if he were given the opportunity. This made her feel self-conscious. Even though she knew she was an ideal catch, she would feel a little self-conscious. She would then back off. She felt as if those men were not worth the risk of hurt. Victor was different. She had allowed him in, but even to this day, she still could not figure out why.

"So, Olivia, where would you prefer to go?" Alexander said.

"Surprise me," Olivia answered.

Once outside, they both commented on the weather. If the forecast held true, the tropical storm should reach the shoreline within forty-eight hours. It was expected to reach the maximum winds of forty-five miles per hour and hit an area about one hundred miles south of Houston. As of right now, Houston was not in harm's way. It was a nice summer breeze; however, the winds were only a little more intense than yesterday's.

"Well, allow me to take you some place that I think you would enjoy," Alexander said.

Olivia was even more intrigued because she felt as if he really did not know her. She was puzzled even with actually knowing herself now, but nonetheless, she had agreed to the date because he was captivating.

"Okay," Olivia responded.

Alexander waved down a cab, and he gave the driver the address but not the name of the establishment. Olivia had no idea where they were going, but for some reason, she trusted him.

They chatted on the way about everything. Their conversation was in sync. Olivia also learned a great deal about Alex, his preferred name. They had similar backgrounds, and she also learned that their paths had probably crossed on several occasions, for instance, when Olivia completed an internship with the Boys and Girls Organization of Florida during her senior year in college. She and Isaiah had just started dating, but Olivia remembered Alex's charismatic style. Just about every female intern wanted his attention, but Olivia knew that he only wanted hers. Olivia knew when she spotted him that there was a familiarity, but now she knew why. During her college days, she had noticed Alex, but her heart belonged to Isaiah.

Olivia and Alex were so engrossed in their conversation that the driver had to announce their arrival twice before either of them noticed him. Olivia glanced up and saw the marquee. They were apparently about to attend a service of one of her favorite television ministers.

"You look surprised, Olivia," Alex said.

"I am," Olivia responded, smiling.

"Well, I am glad," Alex added. "I wanted you to see how I roll in Houston. I wanted you to see what it is like, if you ever decided to relocate ..."

Olivia ignored his comment but asked how long he had been affiliated with Dr. Joshua Christian's ministry.

Olivia remembered how Alex would have multiple women literally waiting in line for him. That was not how she conducted herself, but what she admired about him was that he was always honest with all of his women. They were all aware of his laissez-faire relationships. He was never caught cheating because all of his women knew what they were getting themselves into. Olivia was surprised to see him, of all people, pursuing God's heart instead of the heart of every woman who showed him the slightest interest.

"I have been affiliated with this ministry for about five years now. After my Angel passed, I felt as if I had no one to turn to but to the one who knows me more. I had to rediscover who I was. Of course, the toughest part about all of it was raising my children as a single father. There were many nights when I just hoped for a reprieve. Most of the time, I knew I was simply going through the motions. This ministry helped me reestablish my home again without my Angel," Alex said.

By this time, they had reached the entrance. Even though Olivia had praised and worshipped with Dr. Christian in her PJs wirelessly, she was grateful for this personable experience. Shockingly, Olivia was also enjoying Alexander's company.

"We are a little later than I expected, but I was hoping—" Alex was interrupted.

"There you are, Minister Alex. We were wondering if you were going to make it in time to lead corporate prayer," the attendant said. "You are just in time, and I will walk your guest to your regular seating."

"Yes please, John, and by the way, this is Olivia. Olivia, this is John. John is my right-hand man," Alex added. Alex and John exchanged fists bumps.

"Hurry, Minister Alex, you have ten minutes before we go live, and you already know that Minister Katy was ready to back you up tonight," John said, chuckling.

"I am sure she was," Alex added sarcastically. "I am sure she is going to be overjoyed to see me."

"Right," John said, laughing.

"Olivia, please go with John, and I will join you shortly," Alex said, and he rushed in the opposite direction in which John was leading her.

Olivia was impressed and shocked all at the same time. First of all, she heard John call Alex a minister. The only thing Olivia remembered about Alex in college was his friendliness with the ladies and many ladies at that. And it did not help at all when Alex pledged a fraternity either. Olivia thought he was always too much even for himself.

John led her to the first row of the entire congregation. Olivia could not ever recall sitting on the front row of any church, let alone a mega church. Olivia felt self-conscious. She felt as if she were dressed too casually. John must have seen her expression and assured her that she was fine. She sat down, leaving a seat available between them. John must be Alex's armor bearer. Olivia relaxed as she studied her surroundings. Of course, she expected stares because Alex was super fine; Olivia thought he was finer now than he was in college. But Olivia also felt comfortable in spite of the unfamiliarity. Olivia never would have imagined Alex as a minister. The service was about to begin. Alex came to the stage and asked the entire congregation to stand.

"Let us honor our heavenly Father in corporate prayer. Let us thank Him for an opportunity to reverence in our midweek service. Let us raise our hands and thank Him. All over this building, let us praise Him because we are still on earth. Our work here is not finished ... Father, we thank You ..." Alex began and ended corporate prayer with again asking the congregation to raise their hands in reverence to the Most High.

As the music began to play, the praise and worship leaders entered the stage. The congregation was still electric as Alex handed the microphone to the praise leader and exited.

Olivia was floored. Olivia had never even imagined Alex in church and definitely not in a leadership position. He was truly amazing. Alex immediately came to sit between Olivia and John. For some reason, Alex embraced her and she embraced him back. They smiled at each other. It felt normal; it felt right. Olivia was simply in awe as the praise and worship team ushered in God's presence. Everything transitioned smoothly, from corporate prayer even to the invitation of salvation and repentance. Of course, after the service, Alex introduced her to so many individuals, from the greeters to the first lady and Dr. Christian himself.

Alex noted the time as they walked to an awaiting car. It was the same car that brought them there. "It is late, Olivia, but I know you are probably a little hungry," Alex said. "I certainly am."

Olivia realized that she was hungry but would have clearly skipped a late-night meal. It was 9:30 p.m. "Yes, I am famished," Olivia responded truthfully.

Alex opened the door for her and then skipped around to the other side. He gave the driver an address, and they were off. Their conversation again flowed smoothly, and they discussed everything. Olivia was curious to know more about how Alex's life had transpired from ladies' man to God's man.

The driver pulled up to what looked like an eatery from a place Olivia said she would visit if she were ever in Texas. After entering the establishment, Olivia recognized the owner from one of her favorite Food Network shows. Alex and the owner exchanged pleasantries, and of course, more names were added to her running list.

"Man, it has been crazy busy for me lately since you encouraged me to debut on the Food Network Channel," Pete, of Pete's Texas Bar-B-Que, said. "My wife and I had to increase staff as well as extend our hours of operation, and lucky for you, we are now open until twelve a.m."

Olivia excused herself to the ladies' room as Alex and Pete continued their conversation. This place was amazingly decorated. She knew that Pete probably did not have a knack for décor. Olivia was surprised as she looked in the mirror; she did not see a tired line of fatigue under her eyes. Surprisingly, Olivia was wide awake, enjoying the company, and very hungry for Pete's BBQ! As Olivia was exiting the restroom, she ran into Patricia, Pete's wife. They immediately connected, and Olivia learned who was the master behind the beautiful décor.

"We have known Alex for about five years now. You must be special because he has never even hinted of a girlfriend and has never brought anyone, other than business associates or his family members, in for dining," Patricia exclaimed.

Olivia apparently blushed.

"Sorry, I did not mean to embarrass you," Patricia said. "Pete is always telling me to mind my own business, but I have never seen Alex so happy. Just look at him."

Olivia was looking, but she had not known Alex to look any other way than what she was seeing at that very moment. It was apparent that he was confident, and of course, he was a different person than the one she had met during their college days. At that moment, Alex looked up and smiled. They both smiled.

"See, I have never seen him quite like this before," Patricia said, interrupting.

Before Olivia could say anything in protest, Alex came over and hugged Patricia, and Patricia and Pete escorted them to a more private seating area.

Olivia admitted to Alex that she had seen this establishment on the Food Network Channel and was already in love with the place. Again, their conversation was easy. The food was simply to die for. They even got take-out trays at Pete and Patricia's insistence.

Back in the same car, they drove back in comfortable silence. Olivia noticed that the winds had picked up even more. The driver said that Texas had declared a state of emergency for the entire coastal area and that the tropical storm was now a category 1 hurricane. Both Alex and Olivia gasped at the same time.

Chapter 7

And

We are afraid to care too much, for fear that the
other person does not care at all.

—Eleanor Roosevelt

After spending thirty minutes in traffic, due to the announced
hurricane status, Alex finally convinced Olivia to prepare for
the worst and to stay at his agency's storm shelter. He made contact
with Maria, who also agreed. Once the driver made it to the hotel,
Alex got out and opened the door for Olivia. For some reason, she
hugged him and he held her. She pulled back and apologized.

"There is no need to apologize. I was going to beg you for a kiss.
But I did not know you would be all over a brother," he said with too
much confidence. Olivia knew he was joking and laughed freely with
him. It was feeling a little too comfortable for her. She pulled back.

"So, we will be ready in the morning around nine a.m.," Olivia
added.

"Yes, I am headed that way now. I need to make sure all of the
staff members and their families are safe first before we can open our
doors to the community. I want to make sure the conference patrons

are accommodated, but I understand many of them actually left this afternoon," Alex added.

"And my flight is scheduled to leave tomorrow afternoon," Olivia said. "But I guess I am sure I will get word about the cancellations soon."

Olivia did not even want to admit to herself that she was not disappointed that she did not take her own advice and prepare. She was not ready to go back home—not yet ...

"Well, get some rest," Alex said. "I will see you in a few hours." Olivia allowed Alex to hug her again, and he kissed her on the cheek.

"Good night, Alex," Olivia said as she quickly moved in the direction of the hotel entrance. She felt as if she needed to get there quickly before her body took over her mind.

"Good night, Dr. Olivia Journey Douglas Bentley," Alex said, chuckling.

When Olivia finally made it to the elevator, she heard her phone buzz. She remembered she had not taken her phone off silent after church. She saw that she had multiple missed calls and text messages and that her flight had been cancelled until further notice. Olivia smiled. Before she placed her phone to ring, Alex texted, "Sweet dreams." Olivia set the clock for 6:00 a.m. and hopefully would remember her dream by morning.

Olivia dreamed ...

"Olivia, you may want to cook breakfast because we are not sure when the electricity is going to out," Isaiah said.

Olivia did not feel like doing anything. She had experienced more serious category 5 storms. They were miles from the Gulf of Mexico. Olivia felt certain they would be fine. So, she decided to lounge for another hour. Her family wanted pancakes. However, they did not get any pancakes that day. The Bentley family did not have pancakes in their home for another two weeks.

"See, Olivia," Isaiah said.

"Look outside. I think the coordinates changed," Olivia explained. "I am so sorry."

"Yeah, because you wanted pancakes," Isaiah said, chuckling.

"Of course," Olivia whined. "So, what are we going to do?"

"Well, we have charcoal, matches, lighter fluid, so we will cook our food," Isaiah said.

For one full week, the Bentley family enjoyed camping out in their own home. Isaiah and Olivia grew closer as their nights without distractions grew longer. Situations like this always reminded Olivia how blessed she was to have Isaiah and their two children. They did not have a lot of materialistic things because Isaiah wanted her home with the children, and Olivia enjoyed being a homemaker. They had each other.

Olivia's alarmed sounded. Olivia always missed Isaiah around the holidays but more so when mother nature reminded the world that there was something that humans cannot control.

Olivia needed her daily devotion this morning, and before she even checked her messages or looked out of her hotel window, she prayed. She prayed for everything and everybody, especially those she had just met last night. Olivia knew that she only needed faith in knowing that everything would work out fine.

Minutes later, Olivia had responded to all of her emails, texts, and phone calls. Of course, all three men had texted. Alex's message made her smile. She was just a little uneasy about him. Yes, the attraction was there, but where was this going? Olivia knew she needed to trust God. For years, she had been stuck. She had accepted that she might never experience romance again.

The phone rang, and it was Maria.

Before Olivia could even say hello, Maria bombarded her with multiple questions. Olivia promised her that she would answer all of them once they met downstairs for breakfast before they checked out. Olivia was not hungry at all, so she had decided to visit the gym before checkout to get her mind off devouring Pete's BBQ.

Once she was in the gym, Olivia finally got her mind free of everything that was going on around her and enjoyed her workout in peace. She even had the opportunity to enjoy the spa. Olivia was refreshed but could tell the weather was deteriorating more quickly than expected. Alex's text said that everything was set, and he would arrive at 9:00 a.m. sharp. It was 8:30 a.m., and Olivia was in one of the coffee shops sipping on her favorite flavored coffee. She thought she should have a light breakfast and reluctantly gave her Pete's BBQ, along with the flowers, to the hotel attendant, who gladly took it. Olivia hoped that she would be able to visit again before she left the area.

"Senorita Olivia, please tell me all about last night; I am literally dying to hear all about Mr. Mighty-Fine Alexander," Maria said with a mischievous look.

They both giggled like school girls. Olivia even surprised herself. Why was she blushing? Even though Floyd and Victor each made her skip to a certain beat, Alexander gave her vibes and rhythms that she did not even know she had.

"Yes, Alexander is super fine, but his great physique matches his personality. But Maria, my track record is not good on finding those men who are truly single. Everyone I have come in contact with has had baggage. I am talking about babies' mamas. Remember, I told you one guy was even living with his girlfriend. Even after I found out, I still thought the scum bag would choose me. That is the number one reason I am having reservations about Victor.

"Girl, from what you have told me about Victor, I am not even sure why you are giving him one second of your time. He has had several opportunities and has blown it every time," Maria said, with an apparent Hispanic drawl.

"I know you are right about Victor, but Alex and I live miles apart," Olivia added. "And besides, I am not sure how Alex feels about me."

"Please, you did not see him begging me for your contact information, and not to mention your life story. He claimed that he thought he knew you from college. Yes, Alex is a good man, but I was not going to give him too much information about you without your permission," Maria added.

"Yes, he seems genuine," Olivia said. For some reason, she could not stop herself from blushing.

"Dr. J, are you blushing?" Maria asked.

Before Olivia could figure out a dignified response, both she and Maria started giggling again. Olivia shared with Maria every detail of the evening she and Alex shared.

"This man is captivated by you, Olivia, and I pray that you will eventually show Fiona and Victoria the exit sign," Maria added.

"Really, Maria, you even changed their genders?" Olivia chuckled.

"Yes, I did," Maria began. Before Maria could finish, Alex walked up.

"Well, good morning, ladies. It seems like you are in good spirits, contrary to the weather," Alex said, while hugging each lady. However, his hug with Olivia was lingering.

Again, Olivia was surprised at how comfortable she was with Alex. She knew Maria was taking everything in, and she would probably have much to say. Right now, it just felt right no matter how terrified she may be.

"Yes, Olivia was just sharing with me about your evening last night ..." Before Maria could finish her statement, Olivia stood up abruptly.

"So, I was noticing that the forecast has slightly changed," Olivia said, trying not to make eye contact with Maria.

"Yes, unfortunately, it has been upgraded to a category two, so it would be wise for us to move quickly. I have secured as many vans as possible to transport some of the conference patrons. Some will be going into neighboring shelters because of the large numbers," Alex added.

He looked straight into Olivia eyes and continued. "It seems as if you are well rested from last night, and I will assume that you had sweet dreams."

And the blushing continued. Olivia could not believe she was blushing like a school girl. She felt as if she had to get it together because after the storm, she and Alex would again be living their separate lives.

Once they finally arrived at the shelter, things got quite busy. For the most part, many of the evacuees were directors of storm shelters and knew exactly what to do. So for hours, as more evacuees were transported in, Alex was in charge. This made Olivia think about Isaiah, which was strange. Olivia knew that the number one reason she was still single after seven years was because she often compared Isaiah to every man she met. But Alex was almost like an Isaiah reincarnated. This notion threw caution in the wind for Olivia. She simply did not want to hurt anymore. Each time she experienced hurt, it almost felt as if she were losing Isaiah all over again. The pain would linger for days, and with Victor, it was continuous.

Olivia realized she was not nauseated as she had been during the trip. She remembered Dr. Christian's message from last night. "How can we expect something different, when we do not change; how can we, as Christians, act like a fool who repeats his folly and like dogs, return to its vomit?" Maybe Olivia was a little crazy right now, but the thought of getting back with Victor made her sick. Her phone vibrated, and it was Victor.

The text read, "Hi, J. What is going on?"

Olivia texted back, "Flights are cancelled until further notice, and we are in a storm shelter. Right now, it is a category two but is expected to upgrade to a category four before landfall in a few hours."

He continued texting. "WE? Who is WE?"

Olivia thought it was extremely strange because Victor seldom displayed any type of concern about anything.

Olivia responded, "Yes, the conference patrons are now evacuees."

"Oh, I miss you, Olivia," Victor added.

Again, Olivia was always saying how she missed Victor. This was a change, but was it a good change? Olivia wanted to end the conversation with Victor, for it was confusing her about what she knew she had to do.

Victor continued. "I want to hear your voice."

Olivia thought, *For real?*

Olivia could not contain herself and texted, "Are you for real, Victor? I remember countless times of me wanting to hear your voice. Sometimes a simple text message would suffice, but you never gave me any of that. You always acted like you did not care. You would tell me on a number of occasions that I needed a hobby. You would even tell me, on holidays or on my scheduled days off, that you could not wait until I went back to work. I am not going to call you."

"Well, maybe it is not the best time for us to talk now. Please keep me posted on what is going on. And Olivia, I am sorry for making you feel that you were not important to me. You always were, but I was just too stupid to realize it," Victor added.

Olivia had always wanted to hear this from him, but it never came. Why now, she wondered? For the past few months, Olivia had settled into the fact that she would enjoy her family and friends and devote her entire being to God's work, which was her agency. Now it was not that one man was resurfacing but two. But why was Alex taking over her thought life? Alex came up behind her to tap her on her right shoulder, but as she turned, he switched to the opposite side. They both laughed—not that it was funny, for it was deeper. She felt it, and it was beginning to become real to her as this relationship was beginning to take form.

"Hi, you!" Alex said. "How are you doing?"

Olivia thought about texting Victor back, but why? Maybe, he could see what it felt like to have your feelings ignored and brushed to the side until she felt like responding.

"Fine and how are things coming together?" Olivia asked.

"Surprisingly, things are fine. Even though there are multiple agency directors here, ironically, no one's ego is surfacing, at least not yet. I pray that everyone will continue to adjust. It is a waiting game now," Alex said.

"Apparently Maria is doing more than her fair share. I have already completed my assignment from her," Olivia added with a chuckle.

"In her case, I have too. She is super excited, but I just hope no one throws her out of the shelter, especially if we are in 'the ark' for a few days," Alex added.

Olivia and Alex both laughed. Again, Olivia was surprised at how well the conversation flowed and at how comfortable she was with him. Alex turned serious.

"Olivia, I need to speak to you about something. Do you mind if we speak, privately?" Alex asked. "We can go to my office."

His demeanor was serious, and of course, Olivia's guard went up, immediately. This was how it always was with her, but this time she did not think she was doing too much, too quickly. Olivia felt as if she was doing nothing at all. She was not trying to entice Alex for his attention. Things were just flowing with ease. Besides, she felt as if they both knew the end result. She would go back to Florida, and he would remain in Texas.

"Okay, lead the way," Olivia said. She was clearly trying to sound upbeat because this was how it always ended up. Floyd was honest, but Victor would disappear on weekends and holidays. Olivia never knew exactly where Victor was.

Of course, Alex displayed all signs of a true gentleman. He had shared with her of his importance to only display the character traits that his mom would be proud of and that his daughter and son would want or need to see in a man. He made it a point in his adult years, even though he ignored this during his college days.

"Please have a seat, Olivia," he said, waiting on her to sit on what looked like a sofa bed first. Alex's office looked very much lived in. There were only a few nights Olivia actually slept in her office, but apparently, Alex was a true bachelor. She wondered how his home looked.

"Olivia, this is not easy for me to say …" Alex hesitated.

Olivia knew what was coming. She braced herself and accepted that she would be single forever. She knew she would be okay and looked back on everything she had experienced since her Isaiah left. It was hard, but with God, she survived. There were nights when she felt as if she wanted to give up. She often wondered if anyone knew how hard it was for her to get rid of her swollen eyes each morning.

"Olivia, I am quite fond of you," Alex said.

Olivia had already purposed in her heart that she would leave Floyd, Victor, and Alexander in Texas. Wait, what was Alex saying?

"I know your home is in Florida, but I know we can work it out. I want to get to know you exclusively, and I hope you feel the same way," Alex said.

Olivia was speechless, for only one person she actually cared about had ever said these words to her.

There was a sudden knock on the door.

"Mr. Alex, are you available?" a young Hispanic voice said.

"Sorry, Olivia, that is my little mentee, Jesus. I told his mom to let me know when they had arrived," Alexander said. "I have only been his mentor for a few months, but we have connected quickly. He reminds me of my own son when he was that age."

Seeing this display of sincerity made Olivia think of Isaiah again. What was it about Alex that made her reminisce?

"I want to continue our conversation, but, trust me, Jesus will knock until the door opens," Alex said, with a chuckle.

"I certainly understand. Besides, I would love to meet him, for he sounds intriguing," Olivia said.

"If you want to use the word, intriguing," Alex added. Jesus knocked with a little more persistence. Both Olivia and Alex walked to the door together. Alex opened the door.

Jesus was all smiles until he looked at Olivia. "Who is this?" he asked.

Jesus's mother was right behind him, and she, too, looked a bit caught off guard. Olivia felt uneasy. Jesus's mother was simply radiant and young. Olivia immediately became self-conscious. However, Alex did not seem to notice any of the exchange but immediately began the introductions, giving Jesus a high-five.

"I want you both to meet my friend Dr. Olivia Journey Douglas Bentley. Jesus, you can call her Dr. J," Alex said.

Olivia noticed that Alex's persona did not waver when he introduced her to Jesus's mom, Juliana. Juliana was a thirty-year-old, single mom of one son. She had just received her bachelor's degree in public administration and was currently enrolled in graduate school. She worked at the agency full-time. No matter how much Olivia wanted to dislike her, Juliana was a very admirable individual. Olivia was tempted to feel a pang of jealousy, but only because Juliana had a chance to work with Alex every day. Jesus was ten years old and quite charismatic for his young age. Olivia liked them both, but she knew Juliana liked Alex just as much, if not more than she did.

"So I guess everyone is settled for the night, and it is going to be a long night," Alex said.

"Mr. Alex, I have plenty for us to do. Come and see what I brought from home," Jesus said, pulling Alex out of the door. Olivia noticed that Alex simply melted around Jesus.

"Okay, okay, lil' man, but only for a minute," Alex said. "I have a lot to do tonight myself."

Juliana yelled, "Listen to Mr. Alex. We have a full agenda and more prepping to do for the storm, so you cannot keep him all to yourself *tonight*."

Olivia noticed Juliana said "tonight." Had there been other nights? Olivia knew she should not allow her mind to wander, but she could not help it. And why did Alex say he wanted to get to know her exclusively? Did he want her as his "out of town" woman? Olivia had to get her mind off of everything.

"So, how do you know Alex?" Juliana asked.

Olivia was taken aback by her question. She could not figure out her angle. "Well, if you should know, Alex and I met in college," Olivia explained.

"Oh, he definitely told me about his college days as a ladies' man," Juliana added.

"I was actually engaged to my late husband when I met Alex. We had a class together, so I am well aware of his womanizing days as well," Olivia added.

Who does she think she is? Olivia thought. Maybe she was reading too much into this, but Olivia definitely wanted to end this conversation and quickly.

"I have been working for Alex for two years now. He and I have spent many hours together on that very couch, while Jesus slept in the adjacent bedroom," Juliana said.

Okay, Olivia thought. *Juliana really wants to be cut tonight.*

Maria peeked her head in. *Good*, Olivia thought. God did not want her to go to prison in Texas.

"Dinner is served, ladies," Maria announced. "You need to come before all of the youth assemble. They are acting like this is their last supper."

"Oh, well, I need to go see what my fellows are doing," Juliana said. "No telling what Jesus has persuaded Alex into."

Juliana practically ran out of the office.

"What is her deal?" Maria asked. "It looked as if you were about to attack her, Olivia."

"It is just something about her," Olivia added.

"Well, I do not think Alex considers her as anyone other than an employee or as Jesus's mom. Besides, she is like at least ten to fifteen years younger than all of us," Maria said. "And if Alex wanted her, don't you think they would be a couple by now or even married?"

"I know, but it is like she has marked her territory. She is daring me to cross the line—a line that I did not even know existed," Olivia said.

But deep down, Olivia knew that she would be returning to Florida soon. What chance could she possibly have with Alex? She also knew Alex would try to continue their later conversation, and Olivia knew what she had to do.

Once everyone assembled in the dining area, Alex said grace and led all who were assembled in a word of prayer. Olivia was always moved when she heard Alex pray. She felt so proud to know him and to be a part of his life, even in a long-distance friendship. She also noticed that Juliana made it a point to be right by his side.

Alex made sure Olivia and Maria occupied one of the ten suites. Once everyone settled in for the night, Olivia shared everything with Maria. Maria was certain that Alex only had eyes for Olivia, but Olivia was not totally convinced. Before Alex knocked on the door, Olivia had responded to all emails and texts, as well as called all of her family members to assure them she was safe.

Alex said through the door, "Olivia, can we talk?"

"Yes, I will be out in a minute," Olivia responded. Olivia liked Alex, and she was anxious to hear what he had to say.

Olivia finally opened the door.

"I thought you were dumping me?" Alex said with a boyish look.

Olivia flirted back, "Almost."

"Well, I would take you out on the town, but there is a storm brewing in the Gulf of Mexico," Alex said, chuckling.

Olivia thought he was goofy, but she liked him. And she realized that he liked her too. She wanted to know what was up with Juliana but decided against that topic of discussion for tonight.

"Besides going back to my office, I want to take you to a place where I know we will not be disturbed," he said. "It is where I go when I need a direct word from the Lord.

Olivia definitely welcomed the idea of not being disturbed again, not by Jesus, and of course, not by his mother. "Okay," Olivia said.

She and Alex's agency had a similar format, and they were equal in square footage, give or take a couple hundred squares, but she definitely did not have a space off limits to the rest of her staff. And apparently, in Alex's case, it was a place equipped with many electronic devices. It looked like a man cave.

"Ummm … Alex, this looks like a man cave," Olivia finally said.

"I guess you can call it that," Alex confessed. "But I do have moments where I shut everything down and have devotion. It is imperative, a must."

"I understand that," Olivia admitted. "In the line of work that we are in, we must be certain we hear His voice."

"Amen, Dr. J!" Alex proclaimed.

They both laughed.

"Seriously, Olivia, I would like for us to exclusively date," Alex said. "I want to get to know you on a deeper level. I know I like what I see now. I know I more than like you."

Olivia knew, also, that those feelings were mutual. But what would happen after the storm? What would happen when they went back to their busy lives in separate states?

"Olivia, I already know what you are thinking, but I know this is real," he said. "A few years after my wife died, I tried to date, but the women I met were shallow. Most of them were younger, so we had very little in common. Half of the time, I frightened them because I was too deep, too serious. I purposed in my heart that if I were ever given an opportunity to love again, I would do it better; I would cherish what God has given me. So as you can imagine, I have not found that one who understands anything I say or do."

"Alex, I honestly do not know if my friends even can grasp this concept," Olivia confessed. "I will never forget how I felt in the beginning; it honestly felt like someone had literally taken my heart right out of my chest. I felt anger and then guilt. My emotions would be all over the place at times, but I know, for the most part, I just missed my Isaiah."

"I know. I miss my Angel every day of the week," Alex admitted. "But when I saw you, Olivia, I knew you were an answer to my prayer. I know we live miles apart, but I know we have been connected for a reason. I have not felt such a connection in years."

"Me too," Olivia admitted. "But …"

Alex interrupted her with a kiss on the cheek. "Let me prove to you that this can and will work," Alex continued. "I promise I will do whatever it takes to show you how much I care. Just say okay."

"Okay," Olivia agreed. Besides their strong physical attraction, Olivia felt a connection deeper than she had felt with anyone.

As they heard the winds and rain sing nature's tunes repeatedly, Alex and Olivia talked until they both fell asleep.

When Olivia finally opened her eyes, she discovered Alex staring at her. She was a little embarrassed, for she could not believe she had spent the night with him. However, it was quite innocent. She also was embarrassed because she snored and snored loudly at times. Oftentimes Olivia woke herself out of a dead sleep.

"You are beautiful, Dr. Olivia Journey Douglas Bentley," Alex said, beaming.

Olivia thought Alex was quite handsome. He was even handsome in the wee hours of the morning.

"Thank you," she said, blushing. "You are not so bad yourself."

"Well, Olivia is finally opening up to a brother," Alex exclaimed. "I knew it would be just a matter of time before a brother could cut through that tough exterior."

"Ummm … not so fast, Alexander. Let us not forget how you were all up on a sister and sending her flowers …" Olivia said, grandstanding.

"Okay, okay," Alex said. "You got me, but I will not ever deny that I am truly smitten by you, Olivia." Alex leaned over and kissed her on the forehead.

Olivia relaxed, for it was seldom that she allowed anyone this close to her to even try anything with her. She never allowed anyone to see this side of her.

"So, what time is it?" Olivia asked, changing the subject.

"It is about five a.m." Alex responded. "I brought you up some freshly brewed coffee. We need to start bringing all the directors together to survey possible damages. We actually lost power around three a.m., but the generators have been working fine."

"How long have you been awake?" Olivia asked.

"Only for about an hour. I decided to do a brief survey and get an update on the weather," Alex added. "Even though the eye of the storm has dismantled, the storm system has stalled. It seems as if the rain is not letting up anytime soon. I also wanted to make sure breakfast, lunch, and dinner would not be affected by the lack of full power."

"Okay, let us get started," Olivia said, sipping the coffee Alex had given her. Olivia noticed that it was her favorite flavor. Alex must have noticed her reaction.

"Yes, it is my job to discover what my woman likes, what makes her happy, what makes her sad, and everything in between," Alex said with apparent pride.

Olivia blushed. She could not ever remember anyone taking the time to study her or even acting like they even cared about what she liked.

Alex continued, "And from the expression on her face, I am excelling."

They both laughed.

"Okay, let us get going, for we have a great deal of work to accomplish. I will walk you to your suite, and we can meet in my office in an hour. I am beginning to smell a sister."

Olivia gave Alex a playful punch. He took her hand and kissed it. Olivia was mesmerized. Both Olivia and Alex looked deeply into each other's eyes. Olivia looked away first.

"Okay, let us go so I can freshen up," Olivia said.

"After you, Dr. Bentley," Alex said.

As they were making their way to her suite, they ran into Juliana and Jesus.

"Mr. Alex, I was looking for you last night," Jesus said

"Why, what is going on?" Alex asked.

Jesus started crying, and his mother explained to us that Jesus was concerned about his natural father who had refused to seek shelter. She added that he and Jesus were communicating by phone until all communication dropped.

"Where were you, Mr. Alex?" Jesus cried.

"I am here now, Jesus," Alex said, trying to console Jesus. "Let us go to the cafeteria and see if we can get something to eat."

Alex looked at Olivia, and Olivia gave an understanding nod.

Once Alex and Jesus were out of sight, Juliana had some choice words for Olivia. Olivia did not understand what Juliana's problem with her was.

"This certainly does not look good in the eyes of a young child. What were you thinking? How could you spend the night with a man you barely even know? He is a Christian, and I thought you were too," Juliana said, with an apparent attitude. Juliana walked off before Olivia could get a word in.

Olivia felt her natural hair straighten. She had not been this upset since she taught middle school. Every day she would try to figure out why Little Johnny and Little Mary would come to school with a purpose to get on her nerves. Olivia did not get Juliana. It was clearly apparent that Alex only saw her as his right-hand business associate. Maria opened the door to the suite.

"Well, good morning, and where did you stay last night?" Maria asked with a smile.

But Olivia was not smiling. A lovely evening had just turned into a nightmare. How was Olivia going to deal with Juliana when she worked so closely with Alex, not to mention that Alex was a mentor to her son? Olivia had a lot to consider. She and Alex had an obvious connection, but was she willing to deal with this continuous hostility from Juliana?

"Come in and tell me all about your evening, lady," Maria continued.

Olivia finally calmed down. She gulped down her coffee, but before telling Maria anything, she showered. The water was what she needed as she prayed. She remembered her mom telling her continuously, "Blessings bring greater challenges." Juliana was the challenge. But Olivia also knew that the battle was not with flesh and blood no matter how badly she wanted to show Miz Thang that she was older and could sweep her behind across the entire floor of this fifty thousand–square-foot storm shelter.

After showering, Olivia noticed that she did not have any type of phone reception. She was somewhat grateful, because she did not want to deal with Victor or Floyd. She was seriously thinking about getting rid of all of them. She wanted someone who she could grow old with, but she felt as if she were aging trying to juggle it all. She was honestly missing the quiet. She was ready to go home, but according to the forecast, flights would be cancelled for at least two more days. How was she going to be able to deal with Juliana for a few more hours, not to mention possibly days?

Maria and Olivia joined the other directors. Either Jesus's father was swallowed up like Jonah or he finally made it to Nineveh. Olivia knew she needed to change her attitude, but this was too much for her to handle. She was beginning to doubt if she wanted to attempt a long-distance relationship with him now. How would she fit in his world? How would he fit in hers? Right now, it was not looking too good. She was not even sure if Alex was even aware of Juliana's feelings for him. Olivia's thoughts were interrupted by Alex's requests for all the directors to help. Each director was given a checklist as well as areas of concern. Alex said that the agency's doors would be open until all of the refugees had a place to go.

Olivia was drawn to him even more. But how could she have these feelings after two days? Olivia needed space to think. She needed time to process it all, but she also needed to remain focused on making sure that her assigned area was covered. It was day one, and from the looks of things, it would be another two days before the weather would permit them to assess Houston's overall damage. Even though Olivia's agency qualified as a storm shelter, her agency had not been used as one. Of course, her agency was prepared, but this experience was hands-on training. All the directors were ready and available, and everyone was in sync. Around noon, Alex found Olivia. He asked her to have lunch with him, and she agreed. They were able to get back to his man cave. When Olivia got there, she was surprised to see that Alex had managed to set up a dining area.

"You look surprised," Alex said.

"Well, yeah. How did you have time to do this?" Oliva asked.

"After I comforted Jesus as much as I could, I had a little time to bring this together," Alex responded.

"Well, good thing I agreed to have lunch with you," Olivia retorted.

"You know you could not say no to a brother," Alex said, beaming.

Olivia playfully punched him in the arm. She was amazed at his muscular physique. Olivia was growing more and more attracted to him. Maybe they should not be separated from the others. Alex caught her hand and kissed it again. Olivia started feeling things. She wanted more than a hand kiss. She brought her thoughts and feelings under subjection, as she had oftentimes practiced. Olivia pulled her hand back.

"So, what are we eating? You only served me coffee this morning," Olivia said with a flirtatious smile.

But Olivia did not care what was on the menu, for she knew then that she chose him. She wanted to forsake all of the rest. However, in the back of her mind, she could not shake the lingering questions about Juliana and Jesus, but she knew it was not her place to question it. Again, she had to trust that all would be fine.

They ate and of course, enjoyed each other's company. They did not speak about her returning to Florida, or even about the future of their relationship. Neither one of them wanted the time to advance.

After their meal, they went back to work. The rain persisted into the night, but everything in the shelter remained steady, with minor issues of concern. However, those concerns were handled in a timely manner. The rain finally ended the next morning, which was contrary to the forecast. It was also discovered that Houston had avoided the brunt of the storm. Many evacuees were able to return safely to their homes; however, many directors stayed behind to assist.

Olivia and Alex repeated their lunch and dinner dates as well as their nightly conversation for three days. Olivia finally made contact with her job, her family, as well as Floyd and Victor. Olivia decided to wait until she returned home to end things with both men.

"Olivia, this is our last night together, but I do not want you to go. I know that we have avoided discussing the future, but it is right in front of us," Alex said.

His voice was so sincere that it took everything in Olivia not to cry. How could she feel this way about a man she had only grown to know over the course of a few days? Only if they actually lived in the same area would things be different. Fortunately, Olivia had not had another run in with Juliana, but what did it matter now? Olivia was leaving town. They made the best of their last night. Alex found every possible game two people could play. He whooped her in chess, but she crushed him in Scrabble. They both fell asleep while playing UNO.

They were awakened by a frantic knock on the door. Both Olivia and Alex looked as if they were teenagers who were caught making out.

"Who could that be?" Alex said.

"Mr. Alex? Mr. Alex? Are you in there?" Jesus said.

Alex ran to the door and opened it. Not only was Jesus standing on the other side, but Juliana was right behind him. Jesus ran into Alex's arms, and Alex tried to comfort him.

"Mr. Alex, you have to help me find my dad. Even though our phone services are better, I still cannot reach my dad. You have to help me. Many search and rescue teams are out there; we have to join in too," Jesus cried.

"Okay, okay. I tell you what. Give me a minute and I will meet you by the front door of the building," Alex said.

As Alex was speaking to Jesus, Juliana was looking at Olivia as if she wanted to nail her to a cross. Olivia had enough of this home chick, and she could not understand how Alex could not see how much Juliana wanted him. She also wondered if Juliana had actually told Alex how she felt.

"Okay, Mr. Alex but the rescue team will be leaving soon," Jesus added.

"Okay, okay …" added Alex.

Alex closed the door behind them. "Olivia, I am sorry," Alex said.

"I understand," Olivia added. "Do what you must."

"I promise I will be back to take you to the airport," Alex added.

Alex hugged her in a long embrace, and then they walked to her suite.

"I want to kiss you, Dr. J, but I want it to be the right setting," he whispered.

Olivia did not hold back and said, "Me too."

They smiled at each other. Olivia knew in her heart that she would see him again. Olivia was in love.

"I will be back," Alex said.

"Okay," Olivia responded.

Hours later, Olivia and Maria waited as long as they could. Olivia knew that they had to leave before they missed their flight. Neither Olivia or Maria had phone service, and no one seemed to know where the rescue team was. Ironically, Juliana was the only one available to transport them to the airport. As Olivia was getting out of the vehicle, Juliana stopped her.

"It is for the best. Besides, the ratio of long-distance relationships enduring the distance is low or even nonexistent," Juliana said.

"Really? What exactly is your problem with me? Why do you purposely distract something that clearly does not concern you?" Olivia asked.

"Anything that concerns my son concerns me," she responded.

"You have got to be kidding," Olivia said.

"Everything was fine before you came. I was finally going to get my son the family he has been wanting," she said.

"What are you talking about? Your ten-year-old son is directing the rescue team to find his dad," Olivia said. "Does Alex even know how you feel about him?"

"I do not know what you are talking about," she said.

"You want Alex. Your son seems to be fine with Alex simply being a mentor in his life," Olivia proclaimed. "Alex has been his mentor for two years. What is the deal, Juliana?"

Maria surfaced.

"Olivia, I think we need to go now, before we miss our flight," Maria said.

"Yes, you both have a safe trip," Juliana finally said.

Olivia simply walked away. Olivia was having second thoughts— not about her feelings for Alex, but for the simple fact that she was leaving town. Alex had his life in Houston without her. She and Maria boarded their flight bound for Florida.

Chapter 8

· ~⚭ ·

Go

I have discovered in life that there are ways of getting almost anywhere you want to go, if you really want to go.

—Langston Hughes

During the entire flight home, Maria tried to convince Olivia to reconsider her decision about Alex. Maria thought Olivia was simply being stubborn or just plain scared. She told her that Juliana was threatened by her, but Olivia was threatened by Juliana and Jesus's relationship with Alex. Alex sent several text messages during her flight home, but Olivia did not respond. She read them all. She was even okay with his reasoning for not being available to take her to the airport, for he was doing what they both dedicated their lives to do. After reading Alex's explanation, she loved him even more, but she was not ready to respond to him yet. She needed time to think. She was not sure how long it would take, but she needed time.

Jesus's dad earned his name, "Deadbeat Dad." In the beginning, Juliana and Jesus were frequent guests at Alex's agency. Alex's agency had multiple facets, and one was a battered women's shelter, which was where Alex met Jesus and Juliana. Alex had shared with her that Jesus's dad discovered the location of the shelter and would make multiple appearances even though Juliana had a restraining order against him. It was not until lately that Jesus's father had become an active part of his son's life, partly because he was a little envious of the relationship that was developing between Alex and his son.

Olivia just felt something more was going on with Juliana that he was not sharing with her. Juliana and Alex were not a couple, but to Olivia, Juliana seemed to desire more. Olivia felt uneasy. She had experienced something similar with Victor; with Victor, there seemed to be always someone lurking: an old classmate, an old girlfriend, and sometimes more. Victor had a problem with women in general. He seemed as if he never wanted to let them go and had no problem meeting new people to add to his running list. For this very reason, she had doubts believing that Victor wanted her. She needed time away from them all.

However, Maria tried to convince her to revisit each man. Maria shared with Olivia that her husband did not want a divorce. He had convinced her to give their relationship another try. By revisiting it, she remembered why she wanted the divorce. Olivia decided to revisit the men, but she was hoping to forget the hurt that she experienced with both men. She was trying to find ways also to forget about Alex. She did not want to think about someone she could never physically be with. Yes, there was a connection, but would the connection be strong enough to beat *Father Distance*.

Olivia fell back into her normal routine. She actually went out on dates with Floyd and Victor. She should have been flattered or excited, especially with all of the fanfare from each of them. Neither of them held anything back. Victor cooked for her, and after all these years, he invited her into his home. Olivia dated both men for over a month, but she knew she would only date them. She liked each of them, but she was in love with Alex. She did speak to Alex on a number of occasions, but their conversations always ended the same.

"Alex, I just need some time to figure things out," Olivia said.

"Why, Olivia?" Alex pleaded. "I know you cannot honestly say that you feel nothing for me."

"To be honest with you, Alex, I am afraid of what I feel," Olivia admitted. "I just need some time. Alex, can you just give me some time?"

"Okay, Olivia. Fine, but I know we are to be together, and I honestly believe that you know it too," Alex added confidently.

Olivia was attracted to Alex. It was his charisma. It was when he led corporate prayer at church, and when he memorized her flavored coffee. She loved him from their first date. She was also afraid, but she did not know exactly why. Maybe she was afraid of the hurt she felt when she lost her Isaiah or the additional hurt she felt when she put her heart on the line for both Floyd and Victor. Each hurt would compound the other one and become a heavy burden. Floyd was brutally honest, but Victor was not. But both produced the same hurt. Olivia knew she should be grateful that those relationships did not flourish or spiral into more hurt or disaster; Alex was more than she had hoped for. Olivia knew the scripture well: "His thoughts are higher ..."

A month had passed, and no matter how Olivia tried to find ways to distract herself from thinking about Alex, she could not. She thought about him constantly. She decided to give Victor and Floyd each their walking papers. Floyd understood, but Victor's ego was bruised. Olivia strongly believed that God allows you to see the bad so that you can truly appreciate His beauty when you finally are able to see it. She knew she had to contact Alex. A few months ago, she was getting adjusted to life alone. She was alone but not lonely. She did have her moments where she fought the feelings of blaming God for not allowing her Isaiah to live, but she knew she had to move forward. Moving forward allowed her to reminisce about the times she had with him. For that very reason, she was able to thrive and live her life to the fullest. She had become accustomed to eating alone, and she stopped cringing when she saw happy couples. She had hoped for a special someone, and she had stopped those notions some years ago. The lack of wandering, coupled with the unexplainable peace that she had been experiencing lately, ignited the joy. Olivia noted that she had been experiencing that joy before Floyd and Victor did an about face and definitely before Alex. She could honestly say that she was experiencing the healing she had been trusting God to do in her life. It was truly peaceful to be concerned with no physical person. Oftentimes Victor would put her on edge simply because of his aloofness at times. He was one person she never quite figured out, but today, she did not even care. Her lack of concern played a major role in her peace, and she constantly reminded herself that Victor only cared about Victor.

Olivia now realized she was free. She was free, and she knew she did not need a man to make her whole. Even before she was conceived in her mother's womb, she was complete. Her personality, her character, and even her smile were created perfectly in His image. Olivia had to relearn who she was. She experienced depression and many nights of crying herself to sleep. Neither Floyd nor Victor were able to give her what she needed, but Olivia learned that only God could restore her. No human could replace her joy; it only came from God.

It was early November, and Olivia had procrastinated contacting Alex. Yes, she thought about him often, but she had never gotten the nerve to actually contact him. She did not want to admit that she was afraid. She had even completed a twenty-one-day partial Daniel fast, but she still did not have the nerve to call him. Normally when she abstained or fasted, she would receive directions with answers, but Olivia also knew that when and if she took the first step, God would do the rest.

It was cooler than normal on this Friday evening, but Olivia decided to take a walk and have a late lunch at her favorite spot. During the fall months, her agency closed its doors at noon each Friday. At first Olivia frowned at the notion but was happy she compiled with her business manager. Today she did not even go to work, but she visited the hair salon and was now rocking a Brazilian weave. Olivia loved all sixteen inches of her purchased hair. And she was adjusting to her long, relaxing weekends. She had spent last weekend with her children, and this weekend, she and Maria had made plans for Saturday and Sunday. Although she missed her best friend, Ava, she and Maria had grown closer.

Olivia dressed warmly in yoga pants with a matching Nike T-shirt. She was quite satisfied with her thirty-pound weight loss; she was almost within her goal. Olivia had plenty of wardrobes of varying sizes but did not mind pinning up or buckling up, as her weight transitioned. She and Maria would be taking a road trip tomorrow to Destin, so she would purchase a few items of clothing as well as engage in a little diet cheating.

As Olivia was walking through the lobby, she saw Floyd and his cousin. She had not seen or heard from Floyd in over a month. She was surprised at how her feelings for him had changed; in fact, she felt nothing for him. She waved at him, but he came over and briefly hugged her.

"Olivia, it is so good to see you," Floyd said, beaming. "You look incredible. You are simply radiant."

"Thank you," Olivia responded. "And you are looking well yourself."

"You know," Floyd responded. "What can I say?" Floyd imitated James Evans, Jr. (JJ) from *Good Times*.

They both laughed. It was not flirtatious or alluring in any way. It was wholesome. Olivia felt comfortable with Floyd but not in the same way as with Alex. This made Olivia miss Alex even more. Olivia and Floyd chatted casually for a little longer before his cousin summoned him that they were leaving. It appeared to be a double date. Olivia was happy for Floyd; he was a good man but not for her.

It was cooler than Olivia had expected, so she decided to drive to the restaurant. She was happy she had, for she would have not made it in time before they closed in preparation of the Friday night's dinner rush. Just then, she remembered her first date with Alex.

"You'll love this place," Alex said.

"Really, in the backwoods of Houston, Texas?" Olivia teased.

Olivia blocked the memory. Olivia was seated and allowed herself to enjoy her meal without the distractions of the memory of Alex. Besides, she thought, he probably was with his young family, Juliana and Jesus. That was how Victor broke her heart repeatedly, because he was in and out of a relationship with his ex-girlfriend. She knew Alex and Victor were quite different, but Olivia wanted to believe the worst. Olivia was afraid of being hurt again. Yes, she was happy with herself and at peace, but she was afraid to open her heart to anyone. She admitted that she used work as her biggest distractor, even though she knew she needed to put away the crutches and learn to walk again.

Olivia was sipping on her coffee and crème brûlée when she received a text message from Victor. He wanted to know if she had any plans for this weekend. Olivia was still in shock at every text and every phone call from Victor. For years after they met, she had been the one who initiated everything. On more than one occasion, she was disappointed and would spend many weekends alone and wondering about his whereabouts, what he was doing, and who he was with. Sometimes he would surprise her and they would meet, but for the most part, she was always left wondering where they stood.

Olivia was in a better place now. She no longer craved his attention, but the feelings for him were still stronger than she wanted them to be. He was the only man Olivia had ever allowed to be close to her since Isaiah. She felt compelled to answer him; she wanted to answer him. She had been waiting on this day for a long time. He was pursuing her. But was he too late?

She thought she had made herself perfectly clear a month ago, but he would still send her messages. They were mostly simple greetings, and of course, she would respond because she thought they were finally becoming friends. However, it was obvious he wanted more. Olivia was not sure how or if she was going to respond. She received an incoming call from Maria. Olivia responded with a text, "I will call you in a few minutes."

"Okay," Maria responded.

Olivia thought it was disrespectful to speak publicly on a cell phone at any establishment. Besides, she wanted to enjoy the rest of her meal and ponder Victor's question. Why was she having a difficult time letting him go? Olivia completed her meal and was heading to her truck when Victor called. She really could not believe him. She remembered doing this very thing, but she also remembered the unanswered text messages and phone calls. Olivia decided to text, "I will call you in a few minutes."

He responded with an okay and a smiley, blushing faced emoji. Olivia again was in shock, and she wondered why he was doing this now, after all this time.

Olivia called Maria back once she was seated in her truck. "Hi, Maria, what's up?"

"Hi, I just wanted you to know that my brother is letting me borrow his 1957, fully restored red convertible Camaro for our little road trip," Maria exclaimed. "And maybe, if the weather permits, we can ride with the top down."

"Girl, you are crazy, but it really does sound exciting," Olivia admitted.

"We are going to have a little mini-vacation before the one-day workshop, which is scheduled for Monday," Maria added.

"Do you know I almost forgot about the workshop?" Olivia admitted.

"I guess you have been thinking about Fiona and Victoria?" Maria asked, laughing out loud. "And besides, it will be my first breakout session. I am super excited and nervous, all at the same time."

"You will do wonderfully," Olivia said. "And you know you are still crazy, right?"

"Olivia, you are avoiding my question," Maria added.

"Yes, I am, but we will have plenty of time to catch up," Olivia said. "What time are we venturing out?"

Olivia and Maria chatted about their itinerary, and then Olivia promised to be ready at seven a.m., before ending their conversation.

Olivia was actually excited about the trip tomorrow. She could not even remember feeling this at peace in quite some time. Olivia decided to call Victor, who answered on the first ring. All of this was way too much for Olivia to handle.

"Hi, beautiful," Victor exclaimed.

"Hi, Victor," Olivia said. Even though Olivia was dreading this conversation, she was flattered that he referred to her this way.

"So, do you have any plans this weekend?" he asked.

"I am actually going to a conference," Olivia said. She purposely omitted that the conference was scheduled for Monday.

"Oh, where is the conference? Maybe I can come with you," Victor suggested.

Again, Olivia was shocked. Victor had never suggested that they do anything together and especially not taking a trip. The most that they had ever done together was a few one night/next-day morning trips. Olivia did not even bother suggesting anything remotely similar to a weekend excursion.

"Well, I am going with a colleague, Maria, who will be presenting for her first time," Olivia added.

"I really wanted to see you, Olivia," he said. "I know that I have been a jerk for so long, and I know that I do not even have any right to be asking you anything. I just want to make it up to you. I want you to forgive me and give me another chance."

"Victor, if you would have said these exact words only a few months ago, things would be different. I waited and waited. I waited longer than I wanted to, but you still would brush me off. I even wanted you to tell me that it was over, but you never gave any notion of anything, and now you're sending sporadic messages. Why now, Victor?"

"Olivia, I love you," Victor finally said. "I thought I wanted to weigh various options, and I did. But I never could stop thinking about you. Yes, I would read your messages, but I was not ready to settle down. Besides, you made me think. You made me realize some things about myself and even about my family. Your messages were heartfelt and quite thought-provoking, but I was not ready then. For so long, I was in a tumultuous relationship. When I met you, I was not quite ready to move forward. Besides, many women were beginning to take notice, so I decided to date. Yes, I admit that I led you on. I wanted you, but I was not ready for you quite yet."

"Are you serious?" Olivia responded angrily.

"Please do not be upset," Victor pleaded. "I was wrong to keep you waiting for so long. Olivia, please believe me when I say that I love you. I do with all of my heart. I am no longer afraid to love you and to allow you to love me."

"Victor, it is hard for me to believe you," Olivia said.

"I understand," Victor admitted. "But consider this. Think about it this weekend. I promise not to try and contact you. When you are back in town, let me cook for you. Let me love you, Olivia."

"Okay, okay," Olivia said. "Fine, I will contact you when I get back, but I am not going to promise you anything. Too much has transpired between us for me to consider trusting you now."

"I deserve that, but you will not regret it," Victor added. "Not this time."

Victor gave Olivia his complete itinerary for the entire weekend. He had never done this before. He even gave her addresses and contacts. This was all new to Olivia, but was it going to be enough? She still thought about Alex more so than she had ever thought about Victor.

Maria and Olivia hit the road at 7:00 a.m. sharp the next morning. The weather was forecasted to be eighty degrees by noon.

"This is some crazy weather, but I am loving every minute of it," Maria admitted.

Shaded in sunglasses with smiles on their faces, Maria and

Olivia cruised the highway. Presently, it was too cool to open the top, but the bright sun danced on the windshield, reflecting their radiant glow. Both women had experienced some highs and lows; however, they knew what it took to be resilient.

Olivia confided her entire conversation with Victor. Maria, again, was insistent that Olivia deserved better. Maria even compared her ex-husband's character traits with Victor's. Olivia knew, in a sense, that Maria was quite familiar with sensing when someone was full of themselves. Olivia knew Victor was arrogant and a little cocky, but she still loved him. But she was beginning to believe that she was no longer *in love* with him.

Olivia and Maria checked in at their bed and breakfast and had brunch. Olivia thought it was nothing like a homecooked meal with all of the Southern trimmings. She knew she was packing on the calories, but with her workout regimen and her consistency, she had been still able to maintain her weight-loss plan. Besides, she simply desired to be healthy at this point in her life.

Their itinerary, according to Maria, was jam packed. Maria's family had migrated from Mexico to Destin, Florida, when she was eleven, so she was the tour guide. They even saw other conference attendees. Some were new, and some introductions were established during previous conferences. After shopping and finally coming back to the bed and breakfast, Maria and Olivia crashed in their adjoining suites. Maria pledged more sightseeing after dinner. They apparently slept longer than they had intended to. Dinner hours were over when they woke up. Olivia had been waiting all day for smothered steak and gravy with mashed potatoes made with real milk and salted butter with all of the trimmings and peach cobbler for dessert. Olivia had substituted her lunch with a smoothie and plenty of water; she was famished.

When they finally made it downstairs, they were surprised to see the dining room still open. Olivia and Maria joined the other patrons, hoping that they still could be served. The waitress immediately came to take their orders.

"We thought we had missed dinner," Maria explained to the waitress.

"At the request of a late patron just checking in, we decided to extend our hours. It is a good thing we did; we have not seen this much business in a few months. This is great; besides, the late patron is quite charming and so handsome. He and his friend checked in moments ago. They should be coming down soon," the waitress explained.

"Wow," said Maria. "We have got to thank them once they come down."

The waitress brought biscuits with choices of honey, maple syrup, and apple butter. Olivia thought that this must be what heaven felt like.

The night was still young, so Maria glanced again at their agenda.

"Yes, we still have time to cover everything tonight and end tomorrow with church," Maria said.

"Great, I am looking forward to meeting your family and hearing your dad speak," Olivia said. "I want to know the source of your word depth.

"Olivia, even though I heard the word of the Lord, I did not always comply, which is why I have an ex-husband. The Holy Spirit never told me to marry and definitely not him. Thank God for His grace and mercy," Maria said.

"Yes, which endures forever," Olivia added.

They both said, "Amen."

"And Maria, do not think that I am not listening to you when it comes to Victor. I am," Olivia said. "I have decided ..."

They heard it together—the familiar, smooth baritone voice. Olivia knew the owner of the voice. Her heart fluttered. It was Alexander. Olivia and Maria turned together to confirm. It was him. Their eyes met. He was even more gorgeous than she had remembered. He was closely shaven, and his skin was a radiant mocha. Olivia knew she needed to breathe, but she honestly thought she forgot how.

Marie whispered, "Breathe, Olivia."

She did. She also noticed that he came down alone. Maybe his friend would be joining him momentarily.

He approached. "Hi, Olivia," he said.

Maria cleared her throat.

"Hi, Maria," he added.

"Oh, hi, Alex," Maria said.

Maria stood and hugged Alex. Of course, this prompted Olivia to do the same. Olivia did not want to hug Alex at all. They embraced fully. He smelled so good to her. She loved that his well-built frame could girdle her curvy figure and allow her to feel safe. She was glad they were in a public setting, for she admitted that if they were back in his man cave in Texas, the outcome of this embrace would be compromised.

Maria cleared her throat again. They let go.

"I have never seen either one of you blush before," Maria said.

They both heard Maria, but no matter how much they attempted, neither Olivia nor Alex could refrain from smiling.

"Please, there is plenty of room for you. Are you alone?" Maria added.

"No, my partner should be down momentarily," Alex explained.

Olivia wondered why he was embracing and smiling at her when he said *partner*. Olivia assumed that he had come with Juliana. Her heart hardened. Before Olivia could give anymore thought to this, his someone came down the staircase.

"There is my partner now," Alex said.

Olivia could not see because of the position of their chairs. She had no warning. She could only brace herself. She was not looking forward to seeing Juliana at all. Olivia was no longer hungry.

"Hi, Olivia." It was John.

Olivia was so happy to see it was John that she immediately

got up to embrace him and introduced him to Maria. She did it so quickly that she never saw the expressions on Maria or John's face.

Their food was served. Alex and John had ordered earlier, so they all had an opportunity to eat together. The conversation was like a well-practiced cadence from a marching band with each drill practiced a million times, leaving an end result ... of near perfection.

Once their meals were completed, they all rode in Maria's brother's car to see the night lights of Destin, Florida. Olivia and Alex continued where their conversation had ended in Houston, but she knew that before the night ended she was going to finally have to give her confession. But until then, they enjoyed the night, all four of them. Olivia finally started to take notice of Maria and John and mentioned it to Alex. He had noticed it immediately. Olivia had never seen Maria so carefree and radiant, and Alex mentioned John's relaxed attitude.

The evening was coming to an end. John and Maria decided to walk the beach, but Olivia and Alex opted to just swing. The inn had a couple of swings on the back porch. They sat and shared the blanket that had been resting on it along with the cat who vanished once they sat down.

"Olivia, I have missed you," Alex admitted.

"Me too," Olivia confessed.

"What are your reservations about us? I have given you plenty of space. Why have you not contacted me?" he asked.

"I just wanted to be sure," Olivia added. "Things were moving too quickly. I have not felt such a connection since my Isaiah."

"I understand, but I feel the same," he added. "But where is your faith? You need to allow this to happen. I love you, Dr. Olivia Journey Douglas Bentley."

"I love you too, Alexander Hamilton Carrington Sr.," Olivia added. "But many confuse love with lust."

"Olivia, if it were lust, we would have had sex multiple times in my man cave during the storm," Alex said. "Come on, Olivia."

"Okay, I admit; we could have. But how do you know for sure it is not lust? Alex, we live miles apart," Olivia stated.

"And?" Alex questioned. "Still, Olivia, what is the hold up? Is there someone else?"

"I should be asking you the very same thing," Olivia said, and then she attempted to pull away. Alex did not let her.

"Olivia, look at me," Alex said.

Olivia did not want to look into his hazel brown eyes that matched his mocha skin. She could not understand how such a charismatic, handsome man could even want her, but Olivia admitted that he made her feel attractive too.

She looked into his eyes. Only one person had ever cared enough to want to see her soul, but he was gone. Even Victor could not do what Alex could do for her, and Victor had months and even years to get it right. Olivia melted.

"Dr. Olivia Journey Douglas Bentley, I love you," he said again.

Olivia knew she loved him too. "But what about Juliana?" she asked.

"Juliana finally admitted her feelings toward me, but I made it perfectly clear to her that I have never felt anything for her besides professionalism," he said. "I even asked her if she would feel more comfortable working with another agency."

"What did she say?" Olivia asked.

"She opted to work in another department; she just started working in our Dallas branch. John has taken her place. It was actually a promotion because one of the department heads was up for retirement. I am still Jesus's mentor, but he and his father have developed a better relationship since the storm," Alex said.

Olivia's heart eased.

"She also told me to tell you how sorry she was. She hopes you can find it within your heart to forgive her," Alex said.

"Yes, I guess I understand, but she was brutal," Olivia stated.

"Yes, given her history, you have to understand why," Alex added. "She is a great employee but definitely needs to work on her bedside manner. She is territorial because she has had limited things or people to call her own. She has been going to church more and has joined a single-women's group. She will be okay in time."

"That is good," Olivia added. "I wanted to physically harm that sister."

They both laughed.

"Well, Olivia, do you love me?" Alex said.

"I told you that I did," Olivia reminded him.

"I need you to say it again," Alex said.

Maria and John joined them on the back porch with frozen treats, and they brought some for them as well.

Alex whispered, "This is not over, Dr. J."

Olivia whispered back, "No, is it not."

She gave him a light kiss on the cheek. It was enough to keep him pursuing. Olivia could not even imagine being anywhere else besides right next to Alexander. She wanted time to stand still.

Maria and John sat it the adjacent swing, and the couples talked and invited the morning to come, softly.

They finally retreated to their quarters with a promise to make it on time for brunch before church service.

Alex and Olivia made a date to run the beach at 7:30 a.m., but both Maria and John declined.

The next morning, Olivia was up earlier than she had intended. She was excited to see Alex. She could not imagine going back home and not being able to see him daily. She quickly brushed away that thought, because she honestly did not know if she had the nerve to be in a committed relationship with him. His heart seemed so right, but she had also seen good Christians yield to temptation, and some of them were married. This had not happened to her because she did not allow it to happen, but she had seen it, nevertheless.

Alex was there before she was. She saw him before he saw her. He was helping some of the elderly patrons with their breakfast. She said a silent prayer. "Lord, please speak to my heart. It cannot be broken again."

He saw her staring. He ended the conversation and came toward her. Before reaching her, he picked up what looked like two cups of coffee.

"Good morning, beautiful," He said. "Your coffee is just the way you like it."

"Good morning," Olivia said, beaming. She imagined herself and Alex waking up every morning like this but in their home. She immediately dismissed the idea.

He was looking at her as she thought.

"Olivia, I want to wake up with you like this every morning," Alex admitted.

"Alex," Olivia began.

"Drink up," Alex interrupted. "I am ready to show you how to run, baby."

They both blushed.

"Right," Olivia said sarcastically. "How about I give you a head start, old man?"

They saw Maria and John, who were looked guilty about being caught together.

Olivia asked, "And where are you guys off to?"

"I am going to show John a few of the sights from yesterday," Maria answered. "We will be leaving for church around ten thirty a.m."

"Okay," Olivia said. "Have fun."

Alex and John bumped fists. Maria and John were off, and so were Olivia and Alex. Olivia was glad she had decided on her current hairstyle; her natural hair could not have taken the unpredictable weather.

Once they were outside, the weather was even warmer than yesterday's. Halfway through the run, both she and Alex took off their top layer of clothing. Olivia was trying her best not to stare, but Alex was so fine. She was weak for long legs too. She had to admit he was in better shape than she thought. The brother was not slowing up either. She and Victor had never worked out together, no matter how she tried to plan and set dates. She knew Victor did not compare to Alex. Victor compared to no one, no matter how she tried to make him fit. Maybe their history and his newly discovered interest in her was all that was left.

On the long stretch back to the hotel, Olivia increased her speed. Even though Alex noticed it, he still maintained his speed. Olivia knew he had the zeal to even run an extra mile. She wondered what he was doing. The inn was just a few feet away. Out of the corner of her eye, Olivia saw Alex increase in speed, only a little. She knew it. She knew what was up his sleeve. She was glad she did not consume the frozen dessert treat last night, which gave her enough energy to get directly in front of Alex. But somehow their legs got intertwined, and they fell together. It seemed as if it were slow motion, and they landed unharmed in the sand. The sand felt like a pillow. An instant spark was ignited, and she felt a closeness that she had occasionally experienced with her Isaiah, but she could not remember it being exactly like this. It was breathtaking, yet they were both breathing. It seemed magical, but she did not believe in magic. It simply felt right. Alex kissed her on the forehead. Then they heard the innkeepers calling after them to see if they were unharmed.

"I think we need to get up," Alex whispered.

"I think so too," Olivia replied.

They both stood up and composed themselves, but Olivia was too quick for Alex.

She said, "Let's race."

"Okay," Alex replied.

Before Alex could position himself, Olivia gave a very brief countdown.

Olivia was able to advance ahead of Alex and was clearly well in the lead as she screamed, "Ready, set, go!"

They raced back to the inn to reassure the owners that all was well, but with Olivia clearly in the lead. In Olivia's spirit, mind, soul, and body, it was better than well, for Olivia's heart had finally healed.

Printed in the United States
By Bookmasters